Oliver Perry Temple

The Covenanter, the Cavalier and the Puritan

Oliver Perry Temple

The Covenanter, the Cavalier and the Puritan

ISBN/EAN: 9783744742399

Printed in Europe, USA, Canada, Australia, Japan

Cover: Foto ©Andreas Hilbeck / pixelio.de

More available books at **www.hansebooks.com**

THE COVENANTER, THE CAVALIER, AND THE PURITAN.

BY

OLIVER PERRY TEMPLE,

For twelve years one of the Equity Judges of Tennessee.

———※———

CINCINNATI:

THE ROBERT CLARKE COMPANY.

1897.

The publication of this little book in its present form is due to an accidental circumstance. The matter it contains was prepared as a part of a larger and perhaps more important historical work, on which I am now engaged, and which I hope will soon be in print. Happening to show some of the chapters to a friend, in whose judgment I had great confidence, he said to me: "Why not publish these chapters as a separate book? The matter they contain is only remotely related to that of the main book, and the two should not appear together." It happened that my own mind was running in the same direction, and had nearly arrived at the same conclusion. The publication of this book, in its present form, is, therefore, mainly due to that interview. It is, as it were, a leaf torn from another book.

The chief reason for writing so fully, or at all, about the Covenanters is given in the opening sentences of Chapter IV of this book. The error and injustice there referred to are remarkable, indeed amazing; but it is not too late to correct them by letting in the light of history.   A brief comparison of the record of the Covenanters with that of the Cavaliers and the Puritans shows in how remarkable a manner the former people have been neglected and ignored in the history and the public thought of the country.   If I shall be able to quicken the interest in this great race, already existing, awakened by the noble efforts of " The Scotch-Irish Society of America," I shall feel that I have, indeed, done a good work.

In conclusion, I wish to return my special acknowledgments to R. R. Sutherland, D. D., formerly of this city, but now of Danville, Kentucky, to Judge H. II. Ingersoll and Joshua W. Caldwell for valuable suggestions and assistance given to me in the revision of this work.

THE AUTHOR.

KNOXVILLE, TENN., *February*, 1897.

CONTENTS.

CHAPTER I.

CHAPTER II.

CHAPTER III.

THE COVENANTERS IN THE SOUTH.

CHAPTER IV.

The Covenanter and the Cavalier.

CHAPTER VII.

THE COVENANTERS AND THE PURITANS—*Continued.*

CHAPTER VIII.

THE PRESBYTERIANS AND OTHER DENOMINATIONS.

THE COVENANTER, THE CAVALIER, AND THE PURITAN.

CHAPTER I.

THE COVENANTERS IN SCOTLAND AND IRELAND.

Religion of the Scottish People—The Reformation in Scotland—The Nobles join it—John Knox—The Revolution—Calvinistic Church established—Mary, Queen of Scots—Romish Church overthrown—The Nobles appropriate the revenues—Discontent of Presbyterian Clergymen—Democratic spirit of the Kirk—Ministers poor—Elected by congregations—Church of England—Henry VIII—Persecutions in England—Persecutions in Scotland under James I and Charles I—Attempt to force Book of Liturgy on Presbyterians of Scotland—Renewal of the "National League and Covenant"—Invasion of Scotland by England—Expulsion of Presbyterian Clergymen from their pulpits—Become exiles—Horrible persecutions—Triumph of the Covenanters—Covenanter Colony in Ireland—Persecutions encountered there—Covenanters seek homes in the Colonies—Influence of the Revolution in Scotland on England—Education in Scotland—Founding of her Universities—Education in the Colonies under the Covenanters.

In this chapter I shall briefly give an account of the origin and rise of the Covenanters in Scotland, and of the persecutions they endured there; I shall notice the transplanting of a part of them in Ire-

(ix)

land, their sojourn and persecutions in their new home, and finally give an account of their departure for the American Colonies. All this will be a mere summary of the history of these important events.

To understand who and what the Covenanters were, it is necessary to turn to the history of the Scottish people. The history of Scotland during the fifteenth and sixteenth centuries is largely a history of its religion. From time immemorial the people of that country had professed the Catholic faith. With the great awakening in Europe, caused by the Reformation, there came a change in Scotland also. Suddenly the people turned from Catholicism to Calvinism, with a unanimity seldom witnessed in the transition from one religion to another.

The Reformation, in Scotland, was at first the work of the Nobles. James V, with the advice of the Romish Prelates, determined to strip the Nobles of all power in the State. One step after another followed in quick succession toward the accomplishment of this purpose. They were deprived of many of their ancient privileges, and a number of them were driven into exile. These proud spirited men, accustomed to the exercise of almost regal authority, were not made of the stuff tamely to submit to this degradation. Their retainers, with the love of rank and hereditary titles then prevalent in Scotland, sided with them. The Nobles, in revenge for the ill-treatment they were receiving from the King and Church, joined the Reformation.

In 1542, James V died, leaving a widow, Mary of Guise, and a daughter, the ill-fated Mary Stuart, afterward Queen of Scots. The widow became Regent of Scotland, while the infant Mary was sent to France to be educated under the influence of her Catholic relatives. The French King, backed by the powerful Guises, plotted with the Regent of Scotland to purge that country of Protestantism, to dethrone Elizabeth of England, and to annex the British Isles to France. To aid the Regent who had threatened to drive all the reformed ministers out of the Kingdom, "although they preached as truly as St. Paul," * a French army invaded Scotland. Protestantism had made by this time great headway among the middle and poorer classes. The Gospel had been preached to them by their own earnest ministers. Nowhere in Europe had the Catholic priesthood been more depraved.* The people and a majority of the Nobles

---

* Campbell's Puritan in Holland, England, and America, Vol. II, 5.

were united in the determination to resist the overthrow of their new faith.

John Knox had been absent for some years with
Calvin in Geneva. Foreseeing the storm, the
Nobility invited him to come home. Immediately
upon his return, he was proclaimed a rebel and an
outlaw. The Nobility prepared to defend him and
the Protestant religion with arms. It was a time
of extreme peril. But no earthly dangers could
silence the voice of Knox or conquer his undaunted
spirit. As troubles thickened, he was kindled into
higher enthusiasm. He inspired his followers with
his own great courage. Says Campbell : " He
was born a warrior, and could blow nothing but a
bugle's blast. He blew his blast, and the whole
Papal edifice, already honeycombed and under-
mined, came tumbling down in ruins." Morton
said of him : " He never feared the face of mortal
man." Froude's estimate is : " Knox was the most
extraordinary man of that extraordinary age."

In May, 1559, Knox arrived in Scotland. Nine
days later, the people, maddened into fury, rose
and stripped the monasteries of their images and
pictures. With the aid of English troops, the
French Army was driven out of Scotland. In
July, 1560, the Scotch Parliament reconstructed
the Church under the inspiration of Knox. Every

vestige of Papacy except the name of Bishop was abolished. The Calvinistic faith was made the national religion of Scotland. The Mass was abolished, and heavy penalties imposed on all who participated in its celebration. Thus was established the celebrated Kirk of Scotland.

It could scarcely be expected that in that age of narrowness and persecution Knox could rise above the spirit of his time, and introduce universal toleration in the exercise of religion; nor did he. He fell short of the glory won a few years later by William the Silent, another disciple of Calvin, who was the first of the Reformed Princes to extend religious toleration in his dominions to all sects and creeds, although at that very time his people were suffering one of the most remorseless persecutions recorded in history.*

In August, 1561, Mary Stuart, now the widow

---

* Alva left the Netherlands boasting that he had executed 18,600 heretics and traitors, exclusive of those who had fallen in battle, siege, and massacre. According to Grotius, 100,000 heretics were put to death in the Netherlands under the edicts of Charles V. Motley says the number has never been estimated at less than 50,000. The number who fell in the St. Bartholomew massacre, in France, those in Paris and elsewhere, is estimated at from 20,000 to 30,000. Those who perished by the Inquisition in Spain, from 1435 to 1808, are put at about 32,000.—Campbell, Vol. I, 166.

of Francis II, came back to Scotland, to reign over her native land. She was young, beautiful, and possessed striking attractions both of person and mind. Her charms were so extraordinary that she was regarded by some of the grave Scotch Presbyterians with alarm, as an enchantress, "by whom all men seemed to be bewitched." On her arrival, she professed friendship for the Kirk, and only wished, as she said, toleration for herself. But her seductive manners and winning words had no influence on John Knox. A memorable interview took place between them, in which she spoke of the rebellious disposition of her subjects, and asked whether he thought it right for her subjects to resist their sovereign. He replied, that if a father went mad and tried to kill his children, they might properly tie his hands and take his weapons from him. "Let Prince and subject both obey God." This was eighty years before the Puritans and Independents of England gave a practical illustration of the meaning of the words of Knox in the execution of the grandson of this radiant young Queen, to whose unwelcome ears this was spoken.

At the very time, however, Mary was professing friendship for the Kirk, and a willingness to tolerate the Presbyterians, she was plotting with France and Spain for their extermination, and for the restoration of the Papacy. Under the influence of their great leader, Knox, the Scotch people had become a compact, almost a solid mass of earnest, determined reformers, devoted to their new faith and ready to suffer and to die for it.

Mary, who seemed to be born only for sunshine and happiness, was soon overwhelmed with shadows and misfortune, and after six years she abdicated her throne in favor of her infant son, James VI, afterward James I of England. From the throne she passed into an English prison and under the power of her heartless cousin, Queen Elizabeth, by whom she was at length beheaded. Many as were the faults and crimes of " Mary, Queen of Scots," the sympathy of the world has been with her, rather than with the false and heartless Elizabeth.

For nearly thirty years, the struggle between royal authority and the Church of Rome, on the one side, and the Nobles with the common people, on the other, was carried on, often resulting in conflicts of arms.* Finally, in 1560, the Nobles and the people triumphed, and the Romish Church disappeared from Scotland forever as a dominant

---

* Campbell's Puritan in Holland, England, and America, Vol. II, 3, 4; Buckle's History of Civilization, Vol. II, 165, 167, 181, 184, 185.

ecclesiastical power.   The Kirk took its place, and
Protestantism became supreme. The next great
struggle was to be with the Church of England,
supported by all the power of the House of the
Stuarts.

The Nobles who had done so much to effect this
great Revolution naturally considered themselves
entitled to the lands, the property, and the revenue
of the Church which they had overthrown.   Accordingly, they reserved for themselves five-sixths
of the revenues, and allowed one-sixth only to the
Presbyterian Clergy.   This gave serious offense to
the latter class.   They were poor; their support
was scant and meager.   Most of them were of the
common people; a fact which of itself enabled
them to exercise great power and influence.   When
these ministers preached, heart spoke to heart.
Among poor and ignorant people, words and lessons uttered by their fellows fell with touching
force.   Says a recent writer: "Sermons to them
from ministers well clothed and sumptuously fed
would have produced about as much effect as a
lecture from the rich man to Lazarus on the beauties of humility and poverty. . . . Christianity
came very close to the heart of the peasant or
artisan when its doctrines were preached by men

no richer than himself, dependent for their sub-
sistence on his voluntary contributions."*

The great body of the people also were poor.
This fact helps to explain the democratic spirit of
Calvinism in Scotland. The people became a
power in the State. The Church government,
as finally modified, was democratic in all its
features. It was a government of majorities, in
which all had a voice. Says Lecky: " The Kirk
was by its constitution essentially republican." †
The office and title of Bishop were soon abolished.
The Ministers had but little more authority than
the humblest layman.

And let it be kept in mind that this was the
condition of things more than three centuries ago.
Three hundred years of marvelous progress, such
as the world never witnessed before, have added
nothing to the work of these humble, and in many
cases ignorant, Scotch Covenanters under the
guidance of John Knox. The church polity
worked out by them is to this day the substantial
basis of all government in all Presbyterian or-
ganizations throughout the world. It was the
work of the people for themselves under the
advice of wise leaders.

The ministers of the Kirk insisted that every

---

* Campbell, Vol. II, 10.   † Ib., 45.

man should read the Bible for himself. "The
Scottish Commons," says Froude, "are the sons
of their religion; they are so because that religion
taught them the equality of man." The "Book
of Discipline" declared that, all the preachers
being fellow-laborers, all were equal in power and
that none but God had spiritual authority over
them.

These preachers were called to their work by
the election of the Congregation, and not by ap-
pointment or nomination of the King or a Bishop.

Although the Romish Church had been overthrown in Scotland, the followers of the reformed
faith had before them a long and a terrible struggle with the Church of England. They were yet
to endure bitter trials before the day of permanent
rest and repose was attained.

After Henry VIII quarreled with the Pope, on
account of his numerous divorces, he became the
ecclesiastical and spiritual head of the Church of
England. He discarded some of the doctrines of
the Romish Church and introduced some reforms.
In one respect, however, the Church of England
remained just as its august predecessor had always
been. It looked upon all dissent from the doctrines and practices of the Church as heresy, and
it was punishable with death at the will of its

head. There was little more toleration under the new hierarchy than there had been under the old. Persecutions of dissenters and heretics and persons professing any of the reformed faiths were still practiced under Elizabeth and Mary, under James I and Charles I, and later on under Charles II and James II, as they had been in the days of the Popish supremacy. Under "Bloody Mary" two hundred and seventy-seven persons suffered death on account of their religion. Elizabeth, after she ceased to desire to be reconciled to the Romish Church, in fourteen years, put to death for alleged spiritual felonies, sixty-one Catholic Clergymen, forty-seven laymen and two gentlewomen, most of the victims being drawn and quartered.* So, too, the persecutions went on under her successors.

It is not surprising that the Stuarts and the Bishops sought to strangle the Covenanters, and to overthrow the Kirk. Episcopacy was the main stay of royal prerogatives. It led naturally and logically to the doctrine of the divine right of Kings, and has always been the strongest bulwark of the English aristocracy. The Clergy of that Church, in England, had uniformly been tories.†

Most naturally they sustained their patrons in

---

* Campbell, Vol. II, 211.   † Id., 11.

every struggle to lessen the power or limit the prerogatives of the Crown. Macaulay, in speaking of the English Church, says: "All her traditions, all her tastes were monarchical. Loyalty became a point of professional honor among her clergy, the peculiar badge which distinguished them at once from Calvinists and papists." *

The King was the head of the Church. Archbishop, Bishop, and all lower prelates, were subject to him. From him directly or indirectly they held their Sees, offices and benefices, and derived their revenues. He determined what was heresy and what was not. With the power of removal, it can be easily seen how dependent the Clergy were on the Crown, and what a stay the Crown had in them. Thus the whole Church was brought into absolute subordination to the King.

The English Church, although there may be a difference in opinion as to its merits, was certainly an improvement on the one it superseded. It undoubtedly was the best attainable for England at that time. Such a simple democratic Church as the Kirk of Scotland was not then possible among the aristocratic English people, with their strong love for hoary forms and ceremonies. Besides too great a departure from the old Church

* History of England, Vol. I.

would have weakened and endangered the very existence of the Kingdom, by dividing both the Clergy and the nobility, on whose support the government rested for security.

The reigns of James I and Charles I were marked by constant acts of perfidy and persecution against the Scottish people. Each of these · monarchs claimed to be the head of the Scottish Church, with the power to appoint Bishops and regulate all ecclesiastical affairs. Their object was to overthrow Presbyterianism in Scotland, and to establish in its place the Anglican Church. Under the direction of Charles I a book of canons and liturgy was prepared for use there. Every minister was required to adhere to the prescribed forms, under pain of expulsion. In this great emergency the people rose in defense of their religion. Ministers and noblemen sent petitions to the King, entreating him to suspend the use of the liturgy. Crowds of people flocked to Edinburgh to learn the King's answer. Instigated by the Prelate Laud, he answered by commanding instant obedience to the requirements of the service book, and by denouncing all dissent as treason.

The Presbyterians realized that a great crisis had now arrived; they must resist, or give up their religion. and bow to the yoke of a tyrant. They

were prompt to decide. They determined to re-
new the old "National League and Covenant"
of 1551. At daybreak on the appointed day,
Grey Friars Church and Church-yard, in Edinburgh, were filled with Scotland's nobility and
peasantry. After an earnest prayer by Hender-
son, Johnstone, in a clear voice, read the covenant.
"We promise and swear," ran this solemn instrument at its close, "by the great name of the Lord
our God, to continue in the profession and obedience of the said religion; and that we shall defend the same, and resist all their contrary errors
and corruptions, according to our vocation, and to
the utmost of that power which God has put in
our hands, all the days of our life."

The venerable Earl of Sutherland was the first
to come forward and put his hand to this solemn
pledge; the others followed. When all in the Church
had signed it, it was taken to the church-yard and
spread on a grave-stone, where the vast crowd
hastened to sign it. The next day three hundred
ministers affixed their names to the Covenant.
Copies were made, and nobles and gentlemen, and
ministers and peasants rode with rapid speed over
Scotland to procure signatures. Thus the Presbyterians of Scotland achieved the immortal name of
Covenanters.

The "Bishop's War" followed. Twice the King's armies were led into Scotland, and twice they were defeated and driven back in confusion. Charles II renewed the effort to establish Episcopacy. Under the influence of Sharp, a cruel tyrant, who had been made Archbishop, an edict was made, commanding all Presbyterian ministers to submit to the Bishops, or be expelled from their charges. Soldiers were poured into Scotland to enforce obedience. The Covenant was burned by the common hangman. On a dreary winter Sabbath nearly four hundred ministers, amid the tears of their congregations, preached their sad, farewell sermons. The next day they were fugitives in the snow-clad mountains. They were hunted out in their secret concealments like wild beasts, and their faithful followers shot down in cold blood, or tortured and mutilated.

In 1666, despair drove the people to arms on the Pentland Hills. The battle lasted till evening, when the famished peasants fled. New persecutions followed. The penalty of death was pronounced on all who should preach in the open air, or attend such meetings.

James II, on coming to the throne, "hunted down the scattered remnants of the Covenanters," says Macaulay, "with a barbarity of which no

Prince of modern times, Philip the Second alone excepted, had ever shown himself capable."*

But preaching still went on. In the wild recesses of the mountains, the Covenanters still secretly assembled, still prayed, still worshiped. The merciless Claverhouse, with his fierce dragoons, was ever on their track. With blood-hounds and baying dogs, they were hunted out of their hidden retreats. A body of Highlanders, more savage and alert than the blood-hounds, was brought down to aid in ferreting out the fugitives.†

---

* On an old weather-beaten stone in Grey Friars Churchyard, in Edinburgh, it is stated that, "from May 17," 1661, when the most noble Marquis of Argyle was beheaded, to the 17th "of February, 1683, when Mr. James Warwick suffered, were one way and another murdered and destroyed for the same cause about eighteen thousand." This was only about one-fourth of the time the struggle lasted.

† During three months they enjoyed every license. Eight thousand armed Highlanders, invited by the British Government, and receiving indemnity beforehand for every excess, were left to work their will upon the towns and villages of Western Scotland. They spared neither age nor sex. They deprived the people of their property; they even stripped them of their clothes, and sent them out naked to die in the fields. Upon many they inflicted the most horrible tortures. Children torn from their mothers were foully abused; while both mothers and daughters were subjected to a fate, compared to which death would have been a joyful alternative.—Buckle, Vol. II, 226.

But all through their trials they remained true
to their solemn Covenant. Perhaps no people in
Europe so universally accepted the doctrines of
the Reformation as the Lowlanders of Scotland.
They were Presbyterians of the strictest faith.
They felt the vengeance of Laud and the raging
fury of Claverhouse. Sometimes, driven to des-
peration, they flew to arms, with no weapons but
farm implements, and with no leaders but religious
enthusiasts, only to encounter fresh persecutions.
Loudon Hill attested their bravery and their triumph, and Bothwell Bridge witnessed their defeat
and slaughter.

In 1688, the yellow banner of William II, the
mild Protestant Prince of Orange, floated over
Scotland, and gave peace and security to its weary,
faithful people. The national Covenant had been
kept, and a legacy of civil and religious liberty
had been secured, not alone for Scotland, but for
all mankind. On all struggling people, like the
dew of Hermon, has descended, and still descend,
the blessings of the Covenant. The contest continued, with short respites, more than a hundred
years. The final great conflict, the fiercest and
the cruelest, lasted uninterruptedly for twenty-
eight years.

2

From this school of trial came forth that long list of scholars, poets, philosophers, divines, and historians who have made Scotland so illustrious. The national spirit was exalted by suffering. The national intellect was quickened and kindled into a blaze of intensity. Great intellectual lights shot up every-where. During this long struggle, many of her people passed over into Ireland, and settled there. Some had been banished; some sent to the "Plantations" and sold into slavery; and others, to avoid persecution, had voluntarily emigrated to the Colonies. It was in the tribulations and conflicts to which I have referred that the hardy and robust Scotch-Irish colonists were formed and molded into their heroic proportions.

I now turn to Ireland. During the reign of James I, a part of the Irish nobles had rebelled against his authority, and, after reducing them to submission, he declared their lands forfeited to the Crown. On these lands he planted a Scotch and an English Colony. The region to which these colonists went was wild and desolate, having been wasted by wars and forays. They found it a desert, and made it a garden of fertility and productiveness. By industry and frugality they became prosperous, and soon gathered around their little homes the comforts and many of the luxuries of the age. They were a brave, austere, self-poised race. No danger could daunt them; no earthly power subdue their stubborn wills or swerve them from the path of duty. Their Presbyterianism founded on conviction had been confirmed by persecution. It was a part of their very being.

The Episcopal form of worship was the established religion in Ireland. The country was under the domination of the English Church. The natives were Catholics. When the Covenanters, however, first came to Ireland, their religious scruples were respected. But, soon, the Bishops began to suspend Presbyterian ministers from their functions. "All who refused to obey the Bishops, and to introduce and use the liturgy, were deprived of their cures." Numbers of ministers were arrested and imprisoned for non-conformity. In Ulster alone sixty-one ministers were deposed, their pulpits declared vacant, and curates sent in some cases to take possession of them. The Bishops insisted that no minister should officiate unless he had been ordained by them. In some parts of Ulster, the people were not permitted to bury their dead unless an Episcopal clergyman officiated and read the burial service of that Church. Efforts were made to prohibit the Presbyterian ministers from celebrating the rite of marriage among their own people. Private members were subjected to persecution in the ecclesiastical courts. A law for the "suppression of popery" was turned against the Presbyterian dissenters. Froude says: "The Bishops fell on the grievance which had so long afflicted them of the Presbyterian marriages." Dissenting ministers "were unsanctified upstarts, whose pretended marriage ceremonial was but a license for sin." It was announced that the children of Protestants not married in a Church should be treated as bastards, and many persons of undoubted reputation were prosecuted in the Bishop's Courts as fornicators."

With a strange fatuity, the British Parliament imposed grievous restrictions on the trade of the Irish Colonists, which threatened their industrial enterprises with ruin. To add to the many wrongs under which they suffered, as their leases expired the landlords commenced demanding higher rents. Often these amounted to little less than legalized robbery.

It mattered not that these men had saved Londonderry to the Crown, after enduring sufferings such as scarcely have a parallel in history. It mattered not that at the great battle of the Boyne they had risked their lives, and many of them had poured out their blood for that government which now planted its iron heel upon their necks. No tie of gratitude availed against the rapacity of English landlords; no sense of shame or remorse against Church bigotry.

Wronged by the Church, and stung with indignation at the perfidy and the ingratitude of the British Government, at last the patience of the Covenanters was exhausted. They determined to seek homes in the wilderness beyond the Atlantic "in a country where the long arm of prelacy was too short to reach them." When we recall how prompt to resist oppression the ancestors of these men had been in Scotland, how ready they were, afterward, in the colonies, to fly to arms against little more than merely menaced wrongs, we are amazed at the patience with which they endured their multiplied grievances in Ireland for one hundred years. God had not yet turned their hearts to war, but held them in check, reserving their courage for a larger theater and one of brighter hope and wider usefulness.

The influence exerted on the thought and mind of the world by the Scotch Covenanters has never been fully appreciated. Theirs was the first great revolution in Europe resulting in the complete independence of religious thought and conduct. Protestantism, though heroically struggling for

the same object, had not yet triumphed in the
Netherlands. In England, the spirit of religious
liberty was still in its cradle, and had not assumed
a definite form. There were many bold and advanced thinkers, but no unity of action, no organized movement in that direction. The evidences
of a coming revolution were plainly visible in the
wide discontent which prevailed against the universal corruption and immorality in the Church
and among the ecclesiastics; but, except in individual cases, it did not manifest itself openly.

Let it be kept in mind that this was eighty years
before the great revolution in England, in which,
during its progress, the Puritans (who became
Presbyterians) and the Independents, or Separatists,
first became a mighty force in the State. They
existed before, but only in an unorganized form.
The consummation of this revolution, in Scotland,
through the agency of the Covenanters, took
place, let it again be recalled, sixty years before
the landing of the Mayflower on our shores, and
sixty-eight years before the Puritans settled at
Salem.

In an age and at a time when the human mind
and conscience were just awaking from the deadly
lethargy, caused by bigotry and priestly superstition, into a dim perception of the great religious

and political truths established in Scotland, that event must have had a powerful quickening influence every-where.

Many authorities and facts might be given in proof of this statement, but I cite only a few.

"The Scotch Puritans"—Covenanters—"exercised a marked influence both on their brethren in England and upon those in America, second only to that exerted by the Puritans of the Netherlands." *

"Many causes co-operated to bring about this great result"—that is, the overthrow of the claim of the divine right of Kings—"but it should never be forgotten that the first blows of the conflict were struck by Scottish arms, and that the principles contended for in England had been proclaimed by the bold preachers of Scotland for more than half a century." †

"This action"—the attempt of Charles I to force a liturgy on Scotland—"resulted in the war which, subsequently taken up by the English, ended in the Commonwealth, and the establishment of Presbyterianism in England." ‡

"The English, left to themselves, probably would never have thought of such a departure"—that is,

---

* Campbell's Puritan, Vol. II, 2.   † Id. 15.

‡ Id. 32, note.

the abolition of Bishops and of the Episcopacy—
"but they had on one side Scotland with its Presbyterian Kirk; on the other side, although far
away, was Geneva with the same system, and
nearer home was Holland."*

"Nothing but the rebellion in Scotland"—in
1640—"incited by his"—Charles'—"ecclesiastical
innovations frustrated his schemes upon America"—that is, to crush out all the independent
sects in the American Colonies, and to abolish all
the Colonial Charters—"at a time when all England lay cowering under his tyranny. This is
the first debt of America to Scotland."† "James
drove out of Scotland many of the leading ministers. They took refuge in England, to disseminate
there the doctrines of the Presbyterian Church,
standing above the State, and in time their teachings developed into action."

Says Macaulay: "To this step"—to force the
liturgy on Scotland—"our country owes her freedom. The first performance of the foreign ceremonies produced a riot. The riot rapidly became
a revolution. . . . The whole nation was in
arms. The example of Scotland spread to En-

* Campbell's Puritan, Vol. II, 168.
† Id. 473, note, citing Doyle's Puritan, Vol. I, 197.

land, and in the revolution which followed Charles lost his head." *

We have thus seen that the Scottish Covenanters, under the lead of John Knox, not only secured for themselves political and religious liberty, but that their example and teachings exerted a mighty influence in England as well as in America.

The Scottish people were at the time of the Reformation for the most part rude and ignorant, but not more so than their kinsmen in England. Knox was the friend of education, and believed that it was the highest safeguard of the Protestant religion. Through his influence schools were generally established throughout the kingdom.† When he passed away in 1572, Andrew Melville took up his work and pushed it forward. As principal, he reformed the University of Glasgow, then well-nigh broken up, and placed it on so high a basis of learning that it attracted students from other parts of Europe to enjoy its advantages. A few years later, he in the same way rejuvenated the University of St. Andrews. Through these great seats of learning, the way was paved for the

---

* Macaulay's History of England, Vol. I, 73.

† Campbell, Vol I, 19, note.

splendid learning which has since distinguished the scholars of Scotland.

During the reign of William and Mary, a statute was passed by the Scotch Parliament for the establishment of common schools in every parish, to be supported in part by the parish and in part by rate bills.* "Before one generation had passed away," says Macaulay, "it began to be evident that the Common people of Scotland were superior in intelligence to the Common people of any other Country in Europe." Again he says: "In mental cultivation, Scotland had an undisputable superiority. Though that kingdom was then (1603) the poorest in Christendom, it already vied in every branch of learning with the most favored countries.†

Hamerton says: "In proportion to their small numbers, they (the Scotch) are the most distinguished little people since the days of the ancient Athenians, and the most educated of the modern races. All the industrial arts are at home in Glasgow, all the fine arts in Edinburgh, and as for literature it is every-where." ‡

Says Lecky: "Schools diffused the benefits of

---

* Macaulay's History, Vol. IV, 704.

† Macaulay's History, Vol. I, 51; Campbell, Vol. I, 19, note.

‡ French and English, 437.

knowledge thoughout the kingdom, and made the average level of Scotch intelligence superior to any part of the empire." *

The foundation of the splendid university edu-

---

* Lecky, Vol. II, 45.

A confirmation of what is said in the foregoing chapter in reference to the educational advantages of the Scottish people is found in a recent article by Rev. D. M. Ross, M.A., on Dr. John Watson—"Ian McClaren." He tells how the latter, when starting in the ministry, deliberately gave up a position in one of the largest and most influential congregations in Edinburgh, and accepted a call to a hamlet "lying on the slope of the Southern spurs of the Grampian Mountains, on the edge of a waste of heathery hill and moorland given over to sheep and grouse and wild fowl." The parish contained less than six hundred souls, and the Free Church congregation, to which "Ian McClaren" went, less than one hundred and fifty persons, young and old. But these plain people were an intelligent, an educated people, as their fathers had been from the days of John Knox. Mr. Ross says:

"The members of his congregation were humble folk—the school-master, the shop-keeper, the joiner, the smith, and other tradesmen of the village, a few crofters, several not too comfortable farmers, with their shepherds and plowmen. But thanks to the parish schools—including the Free Church School—which Scotland owes to the noble educational enthusiasm of her greatest ecclesiastical statesman, John Knox, the humblest of them, and their ancestors for generations before them had received an education which had raised them far above the level of "Hodge" of the English Counties. Besides, the democratic Constitution of the Presbyterian Church

cation of Scotland was laid as far back as 1410,
when the University of St. Andrews was established, and in 1450, when that of Glasgow had its
beginning. That of Aberdeen was established in
1495. Grammar schools were established also in
all *burgh* corporations. The law of the Scotch
Parliament in 1496 required all barons and free-
holders of substance to send their eldest sons to
grammar schools until they were competent Latin
scholars, and then for three years to "schules of
art and jure." * And, after the rebellion of 1640,
parochial schools were established throughout
Scotland under the direct supervision of the
Kirk after the model of those of Geneva. The
Covenanter Clergy throughout the Kingdom aided
in this great work, as they afterward did, in establishing schools in the Colonies.†

When the Covenanters, on the invitation of
James I, settled in Ireland (a good many, however,
had gone over previous to this time), they took
with them the education and the religion as well
as the thoughts and manners of Scotland. They
established schools for the education of their chil-

---

had afforded in itself an educational discipline for the members of its Congregations."—McClure's Magazine, October, 1896.

* Lecky, Vol. II, 47.

† The Scotch-Irish in America, Vol. 1, 92.

dren, as well as churches. The sons of the well-
to-do and the wealthy were sent to Dublin, to
Glasgow, or to Edinburgh, to be trained in these
Universities. Common schools were provided for
those who were not able to attend the Universities.
So, it came to pass, that in point of education and
intelligence, the Scotch Colonists, in Ireland, were
superior to the English. No Presbyterian could
obtain a license to preach until he had studied
theology for four years, besides his regular course
in college.*

The Covenanters were a frugal and an industrious people. The province of Ulster where they
settled soon became the most prosperous portion
of Ireland. The contrast between it and the
English and the native Irish settlements was
marked, showing the superior intelligence and
industry of the Scotch.

When the Covenanters were gradually driven
out of Ireland by persecution, between the years
1700 and 1775 and came to.the Colonies, their first
care in their new homes, after securing religious
privileges, was to provide for the education of their
children. In every neighborhood, where it was
possible, in which they settled they established
schools. Their ministers were all educated up to

* Scotch and Irish Seed in American Soil, 260.

the highest standard of the best Universities of
Europe. Most of them, perhaps nearly every one
of them, became teachers in Colleges, Academies
or Common Schools. The salaries paid for preaching were generally grossly inadequate to defray
the expenses of their families. To supplement
this scanty income by what could be gained by
teaching a school, often in the minister's own
house, was generally an absolute necessity. The
Church also urged upon the ministers the necessity
of encouraging education, as the bulwark of religion as well as of the State. Besides, there were
in those days, as in later days, professional teachers
who went from neighborhood to neighborhood in
pursuit of their calling. Few persons living in the
first half of the nineteenth century have not met,
especially in the country, one or more of these
Scotch, or Scotch-Irish itinerant teachers, always
strict, always faithful, always well educated, going
from neighborhood to neighborhood in his life
vocation.

Rev. Dr. Craighead in his admirable little book,
"Scotch and Irish Seeds in American Soil," enumerates twenty-eight Colleges and Schools started
by these Covenanter Ministers during the eighteenth
century, in New Jersey, Delaware, Pennsylvania,
Maryland, Virginia, North Carolina and Tennessee,

and he might also have added those of Kentucky. A number of them, though started as private schools, grew in the course of time into great Colleges of the widest usefulness. Such was the origin of Princeton; of Washington College, and of Hampden-Sydney, Virginia; of Washington College, and of Greenville College, Tennessee; and of Delaware College, and Jefferson College, Pennsylvania. But those mentioned by name do not constitute one-tenth, perhaps, of the schools started by the Covenanter Presbyterian ministers in the Colonies south of New England. In Scotland, in Ireland, and all the Colonies where they settled, education was the second great duty and care of life. The Synod of Carolina, at an early day, instructed the Presbyteries, under its charge, to provide for a Grammar School in each of its bounds. And most faithfully did these earnest ministers obey the injunctions laid upon them. For nearly a century before the Revolution they conducted most of the classical schools south of New York. They gave the free school system to New Jersey, and promoted the cause of education every-where.*

---

* Campbell, Vol. II, 486.

NOTE. Some parts of the foregoing chapter were taken, with changes, from my address before the Scotch-Irish Congress at Louisville, in 1891.

CHAPTER II.

THE COVENANTERS IN THE REVOLUTION.

The term Covenanter—What it signifies—Influence of Covenanters in bringing on the American Revolution—Authorities quoted to this effect—Action of the Presbyterian
Synod of Philadelphia in 1775—Action of Continental
Congress, July 8, 1775, declaring it had no design of establishing independent States—Pastoral letter of the Synod—
Covenanters all united in favor of Independence—Patrick
Henry sustained by Covenanters in Virginia—Action of
the people on the Holston in Fincastle County—Rev.
Charles Cummings, Colonel Wm. Campbell, Colonel Arthur Campbell, and others on the remote frontier declare
for Independence — Augusta County — Covenanters of
Worcester County, Mass.—Quakers of Pennsylvania oppose Independence—Public meeting in Philadelphia—
Overthrow of the Proprietary Government—Covenanters
in Pennsylvania—The situation of Continental Congress—
Decisive speech of John Witherspoon—Covenanters foremost in fighting battles of Revolution in Pennsylvania,
Virginia, and South Carolina—Episcopalians in the Revolution—Covenanter Declaration of Independence at Mechlenburg—Battle of King's Mountain—Influence of Covenanters in framing Constitution—Part they took in defending frontiers in the Revolution—Its far-reaching importance—Western boundary line.

Having described the origin of the Covenanters
and their religious, educational, and political characteristics, in the following chapter I shall attempt

to point out the part taken by this people in the American Revolution.

Hereafter I shall use as far as I can the term "Covenanters" instead of the words "Scotch-Irish." This I do because that term is more definite and more comprehensive. Besides, it has a clear historic origin of thrilling dramatic interest

The term Scotch-Irish is restricted in its application, and not altogether clear in its signification. By the term Covenanters is meant all Scotch Presbyterians, and their descendants, without reference to the place of their birth, or the place of their sojourning, who settled in the Colonies or in the States, previous to the time when intermarriages with other sects became common. By reason of these intermarriages, the term ceased, in course of time, to mean both a race and a sect, and came to signify only a race. This definition will not only include the Scotch-Irish and their descendants, but Scotch Presbyterians also and their descendants who were never in Ireland, but came directly from Scotland or from other quarters to the Colonies. The term thus understood and used will make it unnecessary hereafter to refer to the Scotch-Irish or to the Scotch Presbyterians separately.

The failure to find a term comprehensive enough to cover at once these two branches of the Presbyterian family doubtless accounts in part for the failure to do them justice in comparing their work with that done by the Puritans and the Cavaliers. Scotch-Irish and Scotch Presbyterians have had each and alone to bear comparison with races and forces not thus divided in the public mind. Under the general and comprehensive term Covenanters, my object is to show what this wonderful Scotch people has done for the cause of freedom, religion, and civilization in the world, and especially what it has done in our own country.

Want of space forbids that I should do more than glance at the marked influence the Covenanters exerted in bringing on the Revolution, and afterward in sustaining it, and carrying it forward to a successful termination. The oft-repeated words of Mr. Bancroft may be appropriately quoted at this point: "The first voice publicly raised in America to dissolve all connection with Great Britain came not from the Puritans of New England, nor the Dutch of New York, nor the Planters of Virginia, but from the Scotch-Irish Presbyterians."

At the time the great events of the Revolution were being unfolded, the Covenanters were regarded by Tory and Episcopalian writers as the chief authors of these revolutionary movements.

This charge was brought against them at that day. by the friends of royalty, and contemporaneous history goes far toward sustaining the truth of it.

The Hon. Richard Wright, at one time Speaker of the House of Representatives of Pennsylvania, an Episcopalian and a thoroughly informed historian and statesman, declared that: "The American War of Independence was a Presbyterian and Scotch-Irish War."*

Mr. Galloway, a prominent advocate of the old government, ascribed the Revolution mainly to the agitation of the Presbyterian Clergy and Laity, which had begun as early as 1764. Another monarchist of the same period wrote thus: "You will have discovered that I am no friend of the Presbyterians, and that I fix all the blame of these extraordinary proceedings on them."

"Believe me, sir, the Presbyterians have been the chief and principal instruments in all these flaming measures; and they always have and ever will act against government from that restless and turbulent anti-monarchial spirit which has always distinguished them every-where when they had, or by any means could assume, power, however illegally."†

---

* The Scotch-Irish in America, Vol. III, 135.

† Presbyterians and the Revolution, 48.

Dr. Elliott, editor of the western organ of the Methodist Church, concedes that "The Presbyterians of every class were prominent, and even foremost, in achieving the liberties of the United States."

Of course no one will assume, as some of the writers of that day did, that all the credit of bringing on the Revolution is due to the Covenanters, or Presbyterians. All that can be justly claimed for them is that they were the first great body of men to agitate that question, and were the most thoroughly united in its favor.

Mr. Wilburn F. Reed, of Philadelphia, an Episcopalian, bore explicit testimony to the fact that the "Connection between their efforts" (those of the Presbyterians) "for the security of their religious liberty, and opposition to the oppressive measures of Parliament, was distinctly seen" at the time, and was often "made a ground of reproach" against them.

Again, he writes: "A Presbyterian loyalist was a thing unheard of. The debt of gratitude which independent America owes to the dissenting clergy and laity can never be paid."*

"The rigid Presbyterians," writes Mr. Bancroft,

* Scotch-Irish Seeds in American Soil, 324.

" proved in America the supporters of religious freedom." *

" Indeed, so prominent and conspicuous was the part taken by Presbyterians, as individuals and as a Church, in the Revolutionary struggle that at its close rumors were rife that projects were on foot to make Presbyterianism the religion of the new Republic." †

The intention of establishing Episcopacy in the Colonies had been at an early day frequently avowed. "Americans in England were openly told that Bishops should be settled in America in spite of all Presbyterian opposition." ‡ It was in part the apprehension of this calamity that united the Covenanters, as well as the Congregationalists of New England, in their determined opposition to the acts of the British Government, prior to the Declaration of Independence.||

It was proposed to introduce Bishops into America, to be appointed by the Government as in England. Little has been said by historians on this point, and yet it, more than nearly any thing else, united the religious sects in opposition to the English Government. John Adams said that " it

---

* Presbyterians and the Revolution, 56.   † Id. 49.

‡ Proceedings of Scotch-Irish Congress, Vol. VIII, 244.

|| Scotch-Irish Seeds in American Soil, 320, 324.

was in discussing this subject that the Colonists were first led to question the supremacy of Parliament." *

On June 4, 1774, the Covenanters of Hanover County, Pennsylvania, denounced, in a public meeting, the action of Great Britain as "iniquitous and oppressive," and declared that in the event of that Government "attempting to force unjust laws on us (them) by the strength of arms, our cause we leave *to Heaven and our rifles.*" And on June 10, 1774, the Covenanters, at Middleton, in a public meeting, indorsed the resolutions previously adopted by the people of Hanover.†

On the 6th of May, 1775, the Covenanters of Western Pennsylvania, at Hanastown, in Westmoreland County, and those of Fort Pitt and Chester Counties, pledged their lives and their fortunes in favor of the cause of the Colonies in resisting the oppression of the English ministry.

In New York there was an organization for promoting the cause of the Colonies, known as the "Sons of Liberty." This was called the "Presbyterian Junta" by their enemies.‡

* Campbell, Vol. II, 490, quoting John Adams. England in the Eighteenth Century, 135. Lecky, Vol. III, 455.

† Proceedings of Scotch-Irish Congress, Vol. VIII, 244.

‡ Scotch-Irish in America, Vol. III, 234. Campbell, Vol. II, 408.

Bancroft says that the first suggestion of a Continental Congress, to consider the remedies necessary for the grievances of the Colonies, came from these Covenanter "Sons of Liberty."

Mr. Adolphus, in his book on the reign of George III, ascribes the unity of sentiment and of action in the Church, and the momentum given to the cause of Independence, largely to the establishment of an annual synod in Philadelphia, where says he, " all general affairs, political as well as religious, were debated and decided." " From this synod orders and decrees were issued throughout America, and to them a ready and implicit obedience was paid." " By this union a party was prepared to display their power by resistance, and the Stamp Law presented itself as a favorable subject of hostility." *

" In Virginia," says Bancroft, " the Presbytery of Hanover took the lead for liberty, and demanded the abolition of the establishment of the Anglican Church and the civil equality of every denomination." †

" Our mother should remember that we are not slaves," said the Presbyterians of Philadelphia.‡

But, perhaps, the most powerful influence given

---

* Scotch and Irish Seeds, etc., 322.
† Presbyterians and the Revolution, 57.　　　‡ Id. 53.

to the cause of the Revolution was the action of the Presbyterian Synod which met in Philadelphia in May, 1775. That was the largest ecclesiastical body then in existence in the Colonies. Its delegates represented Churches and Presbyteries from every Colony, and spoke for the largest religious body of Christians in the country. Its ministers were in learning and ability, as well as in influence and standing, equal to any similar body of men in the world. Back of them was as powerful, intelligent, and as determined a body of Christian freemen as existed on earth. The love of both political and religious liberty had been burned into their very beings by centuries of wrongs and persecutions. The Continental Congress was in session in Philadelphia at the same time that this great ecclesiastical body met there. Many of our ablest statesmen and most ardent patriots had not yet resolved on the last great step of separation from the mother country.* Neither Washington, nor Adams, nor Jefferson was prepared for it at this time.

As late as July, 1775, Congress sent a petition to the King, which was signed by every member of that body, in which they said: " We have not raised armies with the ambitious design of sepa-

_____
* Presbyterians and the Revolution, 136, 137.

rating from Great Britain and establishing independent States." *

In this hour of doubt and peril, the famous Synod of Philadelphia issued a pastoral letter to the several churches scattered from New Hampshire to Georgia, in which resistance to the encroachments of the Crown was in substance advised.

This letter urged the members of the Churches throughout the Colonies "to adhere firmly" to the resolutions of Congress, and said: " Let it be seen that they are able to bring out the whole strength of this vast country to carry them into execution." This was one of the first bodies of men to take so open a stand in behalf of the rights of the Colonies.† This letter was sent to the Legislature of every Colony, and was read from every Presbyterian pulpit in the land.

The influence of such a letter upon the minds of a people already ripe for rebellion, coming on the heels of the news of the battles of Lexington and Concord, was all powerful, and served to unite these Sons of the Covenanters as one man in favor of open resistance.

* Proceedings of Congress, June and July, 1775.
† Scotch and Irish Seeds in American Soil, 324.

4

This Philadelphia Synod and this pastoral letter were regarded by Mr. Adolphus in his "Reign of George III" as the chief cause which led the Colonists to determine on resistance.

Little wonder there were no tories among these people in the great struggle which followed. All their history, traditions, sufferings, and persecutions protested against such a thing. Two centuries of wrong, perfidy, broken faith, and oppression protested; the memory of the iron hand of Prelacy and Episcopacy protested; the vision of a coming hierarchy seen in dim outline, such as they had fled from and escaped in Ireland, protested—all these earnestly cried aloud against the possibility of a Covenanter in blood being false to his country in that dark hour of its trial.

The preachers of this faith, from the days of John Knox and Andrew Melville, had always been in the habit (for their political and religious liberties had been wrapped up in the same fate) of instructing their congregations, on occasions of great peril and trial, as to their duty not only to God, but to their country likewise. We can easily believe those earnest men, on the reading of that pastoral letter to the several Churches throughout the Colonies, improved the opportunity by preaching sermons on the great question then agitating the whole land. Stirred by the momentous occasion, and by the memory of past bitter wrongs, we can readily imagine that they poured forth from all their pulpits torrents of fervid and patriotic eloquence, which fired and united the whole Church as one man in favor of independence.

Thus the whole Covenanter-Presbyterian population of the Colonies was ready and united in purpose when the supreme trial by arms came. As the great events preceding the conflicts were developing and unfolding, the Covenanters were every-where active in shaping and crystallizing public opinion around the idea of resistance. Freely and gladly they sowed the seeds of the Revolution. It seems strange and providential how these people were scattered over the Colonies. They were not needed for this work in New England, for the Puritans were there. But in New Jersey and Delaware they were needed as missionaries of freedom; they were needed also in Pennsylvania among the Quakers, and in the Southern Colonies among a people traditionally attached to England and to royalty. And where they were needed in the fullness of time, there they were found. Any one who may have lived in the South in 1861 can appreciate the vast influence which may be exerted on a people, in times of civil commotion, by bold and determined leaders, who, seizing the occasion when men are stirred by mighty questions, lead them forward to open revolution. But here was a powerful race of religious people, encouraged by their ministers, all smarting under recent flagrant wrongs, and all animated by a common purpose to be free. They all moved forward with one mind toward the accomplishment of their desired end.

It was these people who sustained Patrick Henry in his important work in Virginia, as the leader of the Revolutionary movement in that State. Mr. Jefferson, speaking of him to Mr. Webster, said: "He was far before us all in maintaining the spirit of the Revolution. His influence was most extensive with the members from the upper counties, and his boldness and their votes overawed and controlled the more cool, or the more timid, aristocratic gentlemen of the lower part of the State." That is to say, Mr. Henry was sustained by the Covenanter members from the Valley and Piedmont region, which had been settled by that people, while the aristocratic Cavalier members from the eastern part of Virginia held back. They were overawed into a support of the measures proposed by the daring of the great Covenanter

leader and his brave followers.* "During the period between this date (1765) and the Revolution,
Mr. Henry," says Alexander H. Everett, in his life
of that gifted man, "was constantly in advance of
the most ardent patriots. He suggested and carried into effect, by his immediate personal influence, measures that were opposed as premature
and violent by all the other eminent supporters of
the cause of liberty."

One of the influences back of Patrick Henry,
which sustained him in his untiring fight for liberty, and which overawed the aristocratic members
of the Eastern Shore, was the action of the Covenanter people of Fincastle County. On January
20, 1775, four months before the action of the
people of Mecklenburg County, the people of that
remote county, through their chairman and minister, the Rev. Charles Cummings, presented an address to the Continental Congress, in which they
said in its conclusion: "We declare that we are
deliberately and resolutely determined never to
surrender them"—their privileges as freemen—"to
any power on earth but at the expense of our
lives."

This patriotic declaration came from the ex-

---

* Scotch-Irish in America, Vol. I, 118, quoted by Wm. Wirt
Henry, a grandson of Patrick Henry.

treme south-western part of Virginia, where the waters flow westward toward the Mississippi, from Abingdon (then called Wolf Hill), in what is now Washington County, far west of the Blue Ridge, west of the Alleghanies, and over four hundred miles west of Williamsburg, the capital of the Colony.

In this remote region was the home of Colonels William and Arthur Campbell, and then, or afterward, of the Prestons. And to that settlement, on the Holston, Colonel William Campbell, in 1775, brought home from Hanover County his young and beautiful wife, Elizabeth Henry, the sister of Patrick Henry, who in a woman's sphere was as remarkable as her renowned brother. She became the ancestor of a race of great men.* And here the brave Covenanter minister, Charles Cummings, the pioneer preacher in the wilderness, and Colonels William Campbell, Preston, Christian, Arthur Campbell, William Edmonson, and other leading men, put forth their solemn declaration that they were resolved to " live as freemen " or to die in defense of " liberty and loyalty." †

This place, too, was near the Watauga settlement, at that time, in North Carolina, which was

---

* W. C. Preston was her grandson.

† King's Mountain and its Heroes, 381. Sketch of Mrs. Elizabeth Russell, formerly wife of William Campbell, 10.

afterward the rallying and the starting point of the celebrated expedition to King's Mountain under Campbell, Sevier, and Shelby.

Again, on May 10, 1776, a memorial was presented to the Virginia Convention from the citizens of Augusta County, another one of the " up country " counties peopled by the Covenanters, representing the necessity of making the Confederacy of the United Colonies the most perfect, independent, and lasting, and of framing an equal, free, and liberal government that may bear the test of all future ages.*

The first town in the Colonies to declare for the principles afterward incorporated in the Declaration of Independence was Mendon, in Worcester County, Massachusetts, in 1773.† It is a singular fact that early in the eighteenth century a Covenanter Colony of fifty families had settled in that County. While we do not know with certainty who were the movers in that meeting, it may be presumed as beyond question, judging from their history every-where in the Colonies, that the Covenanter people bore a principal part in this declaration.‡

---

* The Scotch-Irish in America, Vol. I, 232, 233.

† Bryant's History of the United States, Vol. III, 472.

‡ Scotch-Irish in America, Vol. I, 110.

One other fact as to the influence of the Covenanters in bringing on the Revolution, I shall
mention.   Pennsylvania was at that time the
second largest of the Colonies in point of population, and Philadelphia the second largest city.
The Quakers controlled both the City and the
Colony. The proprietary government was still in
their hands. Both by policy and religious conviction, they were opposed to the approaching revolution involving as it did a resort to arms. On the
news of the action of Congress of the 15th of May,
plainly looking to separation and independence,
the Assembly, acting under the proprietary government, in effect instructed its delegates in Congress to oppose all action favorable to separation.
This was the work of the Quakers. On the 20th
of May, a large public meeting of the people of
Philadelphia was held in the State House yard,
which declared that the existing government (of
that colony) was no longer "competent to the ex-
igencies of our" (their) "affairs," and that steps be
taken at once to organize a Provisional Convention
to form a new Government.

Accordingly, on the 18th of June a "confer-
ence" of delegates from every county in the
province assembled and "unanimously declared
in that public manner, in behalf of themselves,

and with the approbation, consent and authority of their constituents, their willingness to concur in a vote of the Congress declaring the United Colonies free and independent States."* Thus the authority of the Quakers was virtually overthrown, and their power taken away by this peaceable revolution.

The most numerous people in Pennsylvania, at that time, possibly excepting the Quakers, were the Covenanters. They were by far the most intelligent, the boldest, and the most aggressive. The question as to the independence of the Colonies every-where stirred this people. We can therefore easily assume that it was this people, which by its bold action and resolves, at this critical moment, when the Quakers were discouraging the friends of liberty, helped to strengthen the arms and nerve the hearts of the members of the Continental Congress. And never were help and encouragement more needed than at that time. It is a well-known fact that when the critical hour came for signing the Declaration of Independence many members held back and hesitated. At this momentous hour, the Rev. Dr. John Witherspoon, a distinguished Covenanter, President of

---

* Bryant's History of the United States, Vol. III, 480; Fiske, Vol. I, 185, 186.

5

Princeton College, and a lineal descendant of John
Knox, arose in his seat and said: " To hesitate at
this moment is to consent to our slavery. That
noble instrument upon your table . . . should
be subscribed this very moment by every pen in
this house. He that will not respond to its accents,
and strain every nerve to carry into effect its pro-
visions, is unworthy the name of freeman, . . .
and although these gray hairs must soon descend
into the sepulcher, I would infinitely rather that
they should descend hither by the hand of the
executioner than desert at this crisis the sacred
cause of my Country."* Under the influence of
these inspiring words and lofty sentiments the instrument was at once signed, and each signature,
though written in some cases with a trembling
hand, made the signer immortal. Fourteen of
these signers were of Covenanter blood, whose
ancestors had signed the "Solemn League and
Covenant" of Grey Friars Church, one hundred
and thirty-eight years before.

In sustaining the cause of independence, and in
fighting the battles of the Revolution, no people
were more earnest, more courageous, nor contributed more largely to final success than the

---

* Scotch-Irish in America, Vol. II, 104; Presbyterians and
the Revolution, 163 ; Campbell, Vol. II, 487.

Covenanters. "It is a fact beyond question," says Plowden, "that most of the early successes in America were immediately owing to the vigorous exertions and prowess of the Irish immigrants" (the Covenanters) "who bore arms in that cause."* Ramsay, the historian of South Carolina, who resided there during the Revolution, and who was a member of the Continental Congress, says: "That the Irish in America" (they were universally called Irish, and not Scotch-Irish, or Covenanters, until recently) "were almost to a man on the side of independence." . . . "They were Presbyterians, and therefore mostly Whigs." "One of the clergymen of this race said to his congregation that he was sorry to see before him so many ablebodied men when the country needed their services at Valley Forge." In these Presbyteries, as in those of New England, it was deemed an offense worthy of discipline for any minister to exhibit British sympathies." †

"In the Colonial wars their section"—the Covenanter section of the state—"furnished most of the soldiers of Virginia." ‡ In Pennsylvania, says the same author, the Covenanters "stood up as a unit for Independence," and they contributed a majority of the troops that the Keystone State

* Cited by Campbell, Vol. II, 491. † Id. 491. Id. 488.

furnished to the Continental army. The same
story held true, to a great extent, throughout the
whole country south of Pennsylvania.*

Many of the Episcopal Clergy sided with England in the War of the Revolution, while every
Covenanter preacher was an ardent whig and
patriot.†

" Those of. this class by whom it " (Episcopacy)
" was favored left the fighting largely to the dissenting Immigrants from the North of Ireland,
who were only too happy to pay off a portion of
the debt which a century of broken faith had
heaped up against their English oppressors." ‡   It
is but just to say, however, that since the Revolution, no sect has been truer to the Country or more
devoted to the principles of civil liberty in the
United States than the Episcopalians.   It is not
true that all the Episcopal Clergymen sided with
England in the Revolutionary struggle.   Many of
them were good patriots.

In the " University of Virginia Magazine " for
April, 1894, there is a dispassionate article by Mal-

* Campbell, Vol. II, 490.

† All or nearly all of Washington's army chaplains were dissenters, and throughout the war he attended dissenting services.   Id. 491, note.

‡ Id. 490, notes.

colm Taylor on the influence of the Puritans in
the Revolution, which touches on this subject.
He says: . . . "Judge Jones used the terms
Presbyterians and Episcopalians as almost synony-
mous with rebel and loyalist. This, however, was
by no means true. There were many Episcopalians in both the North and South, though far
more numerous in the South, who openly favored
independence, and included in their number not a
few Episcopal ministers.* If we turn from the
people to the leaders of the Revolution, no such
distinction can be traced. Washington, Jefferson,
George Mason, and many others were not in sympathy with Puritanism, and, although the first
signals for the conflict were given by the Puritan
leaders of New England, none were more active,
nor had greater influence in promoting it, than the
Episcopalians who had derived their ideas of liberty, not from fear of tyranny, but from the higher
sentiments of that philosophy which was awakening
a new feeling throughout Europe, and which found
a violent, but premature expression in the French
Revolution."

It should excite no surprise to find that many,
perhaps a majority, of the Episcopalians in New

---

* History of the American Episcopal Church, by Bishop W.
S. Perry.

York and in the Southern Colonies were loyalists.
The Church of England, perhaps even more than
the splendors of royalty, held them by the tender-
est ties of love and reverence. It was the Church
of their fathers, and for it many of them had
suffered. The members of the English Church and
faith felt no grievance from that source. They
saw arrayed against the government and the
Church their old enemies, the Covenanters and the
Puritans. Most naturally they would oppose these,
as they always had done. Thus the two antag-
onistic elements drifted apart.

It is easy to conceive how many true and patriotic
men in 1775 and 1776 might be honestly opposed
to separation from England. Like Mr. Jefferson,
they may very sincerely have preferred the English
government, properly limited, to any other in the
world. The establishment of a new government
was an experiment. The wisest forecast could not
tell how it would turn out. Good men may well
have hesitated at the greatest and the boldest step
ever taken by a people.

Men may, and do often conscientiously, differ in
opinion upon vital questions. In 1861, such men
as General Sam Houston, Mr. James L. Pettigrew,
the noted lawyer of South Carolina, John Minor
Botts, and Governor William B. Campbell, Justice

John Catron, Return J. Meigs, Hon. John Trimble, and many others, all distinguished for their exalted virtues, differed from a vast majority of the people of their section as to separation from the national union. Who shall say that these men were not honest in their course?.

Let it be distinctly understood that the course of the Episcopalians in the Revolution is not referred to by way of adverse criticism, but only for the purpose of showing how important the services of the Covenanters were in that great conflict in maintaining the cause of Independence. Whatever that course may have been, the Church should not be held to a strict accountability for it, since it is undeniably true that it is to-day as faithful to the principles on which our institutions were founded as any Church organization in existence.

It is well, and for one I am glad, that the Episcopal Church exists in this country. It is one of · the great balance-wheels in our complex machinery of popular government and popular thought. On all important moral questions, its intelligent constituents are abreast of the best thought of the world. It is, and always has been, like the Presbyterian Church, highly conservative in its principles and in its course.

This conservatism, at all times beneficial in a

country governed by ideas and not by force, may in the future, possibly in the near future, prove one of the great bulwarks against the tide of lawlessness, anarchy and red-handed socialism which threaten the peace of the country, the security of private property, and the very integrity of the Constitution itself.

We cheerfully pay the homage of sincere respect to this august Church, venerable for its comparatively great age, its conspicuous history, and its many noble deeds; venerable on account of its long line of learned and eminent adherents, and still more venerable on account of the piety and consecration of the many distinguished men who have shed luster on its annals. While there may be much in its earlier history to condemn, there is in its later years much to admire and to praise; much that has blessed mankind and made the world better.

One of the boldest declarations made anywhere in the Colonies was that of the Covenanters of Mecklenburg County, North Carolina, in May, 1775, a little over thirteen months before the decisive action of the Continental Congress at Philadelphia, in 1776. No one of the Colonies was more stirred by the great events of 1775 than North Carolina. Her people were not at that time

greatly oppressed, yet they were perhaps the ripest
for revolution of any people in America.   There
had settled that large population of Covenanters
who knew from tradition or experience the monstrous wrongs of tyrants.   Mecklenburg County
was occupied entirely by these determined people.
When, therefore, they learned, in May, 1775, that
Parliament had declared the Colonies in a state of
revolt, they knew that the great crisis had come.
They did not wait for the action of the Continental
Congress, nor for that of. their own Provincial
Legislature.   They met in Charlotte to take coun-
sel together.   While in session, the news came
that patriot blood had been shed at Lexington and
Concord.   The meeting was addressed by Hezekiah
J. Balch, a Covenanter Presbyterian minister, and
by Dr. Ephraim Brevard and William Kennon.
Resolutions were offered by Dr. Brevard and
adopted, the second and third of which are here
inserted:

" 2. Resolved, That we, the citizens of Mecklenburg County, do hereby dissolve the political bonds
which have connected us with the mother country,
and absolve ourselves from all allegiance to the
British Crown, adjuring all political connection with
a nation that has wantonly trampled on our rights

and liberties, and inhumanly shed the innocent
blood of Americans at Lexington and Concord."

"3. Resolved, That we do hereby declare ourselves a free and independent people; that we are,
and of right ought to be, a sovereign and self-
governed people under the power of God and the
General Congress, to the maintenance of which
independence we solemnly pledge to each other
our mutual co-operation, our lives, our fortunes, and
our most sacred honor." All honor to the memory
of the brave Covenanters of North Carolina.*

The most daring battle of the Revolution, and

---

* In an address before the Scotch-Irish Congress at Louisville in 1891, referring to the Mecklenburg Declaration of Independence, I spoke of the "disputed declaration of May 20,"
and of the "unquestionably authentic resolutions of May 31."
Recently I have read the address of George W. Graham, M.D.,
before the Scotch-Irish Congress, at Lexington, Virginia, in
June, 1895, printed in volume seven, reviewing the whole
history of the controversy in reference to the celebrated
"Mecklenburg Declaration of Independence." In this very
able and critical address much new light is thrown on the
subject. If the writer does not establish beyond question the
authenticity of the resolutions claimed for May 20, 1775, he
certainly leaves less room for doubt on this point than has
hitherto existed. I have accordingly adopted that view of the
question in the text of this work. Before reading this address
I had always regarded the claim in behalf of the authenticity
of the resolutions of May 20th as very questionable.

the most important victory in its consequences, were the battle and the victory of King's Mountain ; excepting only the victories of General George Rogers Clarke in the north-west. History has been tardy and niggardly in its treatment of this important historical fact. In some of our early histories less space was given to it than to the celebrated adventure of Israel Putnam with a wolf. It is only quite recently and since the appearance of Draper's exhaustive book, entitled " King's Mountain and its Heroes," and since the discussion of this battle in the Scotch-Irish Congresses, that any other than local interest has been awakened, in one of the most important incidents of the Revolutionary War. Draper does not develop the prominent part played in this brilliant affair by the Covenanter stock. To rescue from oblivion the glory of this people, in this thrilling event, has been reserved for their kindred and descendants after more than a century had passed away. For the fact is undeniable that it was this people, in the main, which fought this battle and won this victory. The great body of the army was composed of Covenanters from South-western Virginia, Eastern Tennessee and from the western Counties of North Carolina, with a few men from South Carolina and Georgia. It is true that the two noted leaders who originated the expedition, John Sevier and Isaac Shelby were not Covenanters, but that matters not, as their officers and the army were mostly of that people. Certainly Campbell and McDowell were Covenanters, and probably also Cleveland, Hambright, Clarke, Williams, Lacy and Winston.

When the dreadful conflict of arms came on, the settlers on the Watauga, the Nolichucky and the Holston were remote from danger and secure in their peaceable homes, except from Indian attacks. But they were not indifferent to the fate of their kindred beyond the mountains. After General Gates' defeat at Camden, General McDowell who now commanded in Western North Carolina, retired across the mountains to the back country. The army was broken up. Colonel Ferguson, with his elated army, marched into North Carolina, after the defeat of Gates, and took position at Gilbert Town. From this place he sent a threatening message to Sevier and Shelby. On receipt of this message Shelby rode at once to consult with Sevier. They agreed to call out a part of their respective commands, and march, surprise and destroy Ferguson before he was aware of their movement. Colonel Shelby was to secure the co-operation of Colonel Campbell, who commanded in Washington County,

Virginia, just beyond the State line. Colonel
Sevier was to raise the money for the expedition.
He tried to borrow it on his own account, but
there was none in the settlement. He went to John
Adair, entry-taker for the district, who is believed
to have been a Covenanter, and representing to
him the importance of getting the use of the
public money in his hands, pledged him that the
act should be legalized. Adair replied: " If the
enemy, by its use, be driven from the country, I
can trust that country to justify and vindicate my
conduct. Take it!"—a reply worthy of a Roman
in the best days of the Republic.

The whole military force of the settlements at
that time was less than a thousand men. Sevier
and Shelby each selected from their commands two
hundred and forty men, consisting of the young
and vigorous, leaving those who were less so to defend the settlements. Not another man could be
safely spared. On the 25th of September, 1780,
the forces assembled at Sycamore Shoals, on the
Watauga. Campbell came from Virginia with
four hundred men, and McDowell was there with
a few of his refugee soldiers. Sevier and Shelby
were there with their contingents. " With the exception," says Ramsey, a historian of Tennessee,
" of the few colonists on the distant Cumberland,

the entire military force of what is now Tennessee was assembled at Sycamore Shoals. Scarcely a single gunman remained that day at home." The aged were there to cheer and encourage; the mothers, the wives, the sisters, to say farewell. "Never," says Ramsey, "did mountain recess contain within it a loftier or more enlarged patriotism; never a cooler or more determined courage." On the morning of the 26th, the men were drawn up in a body by the direction of the officers, for the purpose of invoking the divine protection. The Rev. Samuel Doak, one of the Covenanter pioneer preachers, was there, from his church and school at Salem, twenty-five miles distant. He offered a fervent prayer for the safety and success of the expedition, and in a few patriotic remarks he closed with the words: "The sword of the Lord and of Gideon;" and these sturdy Scotch-Irish Presbyterians, leaning on their rifles, shouted in patriotic acclaim: "The sword of the Lord and of our Gideons."*

The battle of King's Mountain is totally unlike any other in our history. It was the voluntary uprising of a patriotic people, rushing to arms to aid their distant kindred, when their own homes were hourly menaced with danger from fierce savages.

---

* King's Mountain and its Heroes.

There was no one in chief command except by consent, and no one entitled to the chief command,
Colonel Campbell commanding by the agreement
of the chief officers.   They served without pay or
the hope of pay.   Their march lay through an un-
inhabited mountain wilderness, with no roads and
with scarcely a trail.   These mountains are the
loftiest east of the great Rockies.   The distance to
the enemy, by the circuitous routes the little army
had to take, was perhaps two hundred miles or
more.   On the way, the expedition was joined by
small forces under the command respectively of
Colonels Cleveland, Winston, Hambright, and
Major Chronicle, of North Carolina, and by those
under Colonel Williams, of South Carolina, thus
swelling the total number to eighteen hundred men.
Senator Vance's grandfather, as he relates, voluntarily joined the patriots on the way.

Two days before the battle, the little army
halted.   The officers selected the best men and
horses, and with these, amounting to nine hundred
and ten men, they determined to make a forced
march to overtake Ferguson, leaving the others
on the jaded horses and on foot to follow.   For
twenty-six hours these brave men were in the sad-
dle, without sleep, and with little to eat, and some
of them without any thing, marching through a

drenching rain. On the 7th of October, 1780, they found Ferguson posted on King's Mountain with eleven hundred men, part of them British regulars. Galloping forward to within a short distance of the enemy, the patriots alighted, tied their horses, and hurriedly arranged themselves in order of battle. They were to attack simultaneously on the four sides of the mountain, and thus surround Ferguson. They were arranged in four columns, two on either side of the mountain, led respectively by Colonels Campbell and Sevier on the right and Shelby and Cleveland on the left. When the columns arrived at their several positions, with a loud yell, they dashed up the craggy mountain, and encircled it with a sheet of living fire. The crest was swept by their rifles as if by a tempest. The late eloquent Bailie Peyton, of Tennessee, said of this battle: "When that conflict began, the mountain appeared volcanic; there flashed along its summit and around its base, and up its sides, one long, sulphurous blaze." Three times were the forces of Campbell and Shelby in turn driven down the mountain by bayonet charges, and three times were they rallied and led back to the fight. Ferguson, seeing that all was lost, with a few of his officers, attempted to cut his way out, but was shot down by Sevier's men, pierced by half a dozen bullets.

The battle lasted one hour and five minutes. During that terrible hour, two hundred and twenty of the enemy had closed their eyes in death, one hundred and eighty were wounded, and either six or seven hundred (the authorities differ on this point) were taken prisoners. Every man present was either killed, wounded, or captured. I think, therefore, I am justified in saying that this was the most daring as well as the most thrilling achievement of the Revolutionary war, fought almost exclusively by the Covenanter race. Nor was the victory less signal in its consequences. At that time, Cornwallis was on a triumphant march through North Carolina to Virginia. Charleston and Savannah had fallen. Lincoln had lost his entire army. Gates had been defeated at Camden. All Georgia and South Carolina had yielded to British arms. There was no organized force in the Southern States capable of withstanding for an hour the victorious army of Cornwallis. There was universal gloom throughout the Colonies. The best patriots were in despair. The news, therefore, of this victory came like a great light in the midst of profound darkness. It was the sound of triumph, the rift in the dark cloud, the breaking of morning. Mr. Jefferson said : "It was the

6

joyful annunciation of that turn in the tide of success that terminated the Revolutionary War with the seal of our Independence." The very night Cornwallis heard of it, he commenced a hasty retreat back into South Carolina. From that day the patriot cause grew brighter and brighter until the perfect day dawned at Yorktown.

There were other races engaged in this battle; but as the Covenanters constituted a majority of the early settlers, I speak of them in general terms simply to indicate the leading stock. One of the great leaders in these military operations, John Sevier, was a Huguenot, and Shelby, another leader, was of Welsh origin. But James Robertson, one of the foremost men in the early Watauga settlement, and afterward the founder and defender of the Cumberland Colony, was a Covenanter by descent.

In the formation of the Constitution of the United States, which Mr. Gladstone declares " the most wonderful work ever struck off at a given time by the brain and purpose of man," * the four most conspicuous men, perhaps, in that great work were Alexander Hamilton, James Madison, John Rutledge, of South Carolina, and James Wilson, of Pennsylvania. Three of these were of Covenanter

* Scotch-Irish in America, Vol. III, 115.

blood, and Mr. Madison, the fourth, learned his political lessons from John Witherspoon. After a full discussion in the Convention of the principles to be embodied in the Constitution, Mr. Rutledge was appointed Chairman of a Committee of five to make the first draft of this wonderful instrument, which he did. Rutledge and Wilson were both men of marked ability. Madison's fame is too well established to need additional praise. As to Hamilton, intellectually, he was the master-spirit of his time in this country. The celebrated Prince De Talleyrand, who knew all the noted men of his day, both in this country and in Europe, said that the greatest men he had known were Napoleon, Fox, and Hamilton, and that Hamilton was unquestionably the greatest of these.*

The part taken by the Covenanters of the frontiers in fighting the battles of the Revolution in North and South Carolina only constituted a part of their patriotic work. Every-where along the Western frontier from Georgia to Canada, and notably so in Tennessee and Kentucky, a constant Indian warfare blazed along the borders from the day the pioneers set foot on the virgin soil till long after the close of the war.

The far-reaching importance of this Indian

* Memoirs of Prince De Talleyrand.

fighting has not been, and is not now, half appreciated. But few men ever think that when Sevier
and Robertson and Boone and Kenton were repel-
ling Indian attacks, or invading the Indian Country, they were doing any thing more than protect-
ing the white settlements; whereas they were, in
fact, unconsciously to themselves, fighting the very
battles of the Revolution. The same great power
which put in motion the armies of Clinton and
Cornwallis for the subjugation of the Colonies
along the Atlantic, and encircled them with a line
of fire, also set in motion the fierce savage nations
from Canada to Florida, bent on the destruction
of all the infant settlements west of the Alleghanies and the Blue Ridge. Official records show
that it was as much the policy of the British ministry to destroy these settlements, and exterminate
the settlers or drive them east of the Alleghanies,
as it was to destroy the army of Washington.
Both were parts of the same cruel war, the same
scheme of subjugation. British agents, shrewd
and heartless, with a plentiful supply of gold and
presents, arms and ammunition, were kept at work
among all the tribes east of the Mississippi, stirring
them up to their work of blood. Henry Hamilton,
Lieutenant-Governor of Canada, with headquarters
at Detroit, was at the head of this diabolical move-

ment. There was a regular organized plan of operation. Nor did the infamy stop here. Besides alluring the savages with presents, their cupidity and ferocity were still further stimulated by purchasing from them the scalps they had taken. The instructions given by the home government were to destroy the settlers or drive them east of the Alleghanies.

In pursuance of this comprehensive plan, the Indians north of the Ohio made unceasing war on the settlers around Pittsburg and on those in Kentucky. Those south of the Ohio harrassed and threatened the settlements on the Cumberland, and attempted over and over again to destroy the Holston, the Watauga, and the Nolichucky people. So, also, the frontiers of the Southern Colonies were harrassed by these fierce allies of England. Again and again these demons, incited by British agents, silently and murderously crept through the dark forests, to fall on the settlements with fire and tomahawk and scalping-knife, sparing neither age nor sex. And as often, the leaders of the settlements—Evan Shelby, Christian, Robertson, Boone, Kenton, Logan, and Todd, and notably Sevier and Clarke—led expeditions into the homes of the savages and inflicted on them merited chastisement. So, at the close of the Revolution, not a settlement west of the mountains had been destroyed, not an inch of territory had been lost. Under the leadership of Sevier, the Watauga, the Holston, and the Nolichucky settlers had slowly crept down these streams, extending the settlements further and further west. Robertson had firmly planted his colony on the Cumberland and in the heart of Middle Tennessee. Boone, Logan, and others had successfully defended Kentucky, though more than once narrowly escaping destruction. And General George Rogers Clarke, by a series of exploits almost unparalleled for daring, had conquered and firmly held Illinois and Indiana.

And now came peace. Where should the western boundary line be fixed? Spain had been our ally in the late war. She owned vast possessions west of the Mississippi. Forecasting the growth and expansion of this young republic, and foreseeing dangers to her western possessions, she naturally sought to restrict our territory by making the Alleghanies the boundary. France had also been our faithful ally. She insisted that the line should be so fixed as to include the country around the head-waters of the Tennessee, covering Eastern Tennessee, and that between the Ohio and the Cumberland, thus restoring to England a large part of Tennessee and the territory now forming the States of Alabama and Mississippi, and all the great region afterward known as the North-west Territory. Strange to say, the Continental Congress, in a chivalric spirit of gratitude and courtesy toward its late allies, had instructed our commissioners, in fixing the boundary, to respect the wishes of France in that respect. Franklin wished to obey these instructions, but Jay was immovable in demanding the Mississippi as the western boundary. Adams sided with him, and England yielding, the eastern bank of that river for the most of its length became our western boundary.

It thus appears that while the Continental armies barely held the Atlantic States against the British fleet and armies, a few hundred hunters and pioneers of Tennessee, Kentucky, Western Pennsylvania and South-western Virginia, mostly Covenanters, unaided by Congress, and acting at their on expense and on their own volition, won and held by their valor what has proved to be the very heart of our great empire, against the combined power of all the savage nations between Canada and Florida, backed by British agents, stimulated by British gold, and aided sometimes by British troops. Putting out of view entirely the services rendered to the cause of Independence by Sevier and his associates at King's Mountain, and in other battles in the South, it is manifest that the Indian battles on the frontier were as important to the lasting power and greatness of our country as were the battles of Washington and Greene. The frontier leaders occupied, won and held the territory now covered by the great States of Tennessee, Alabama, Mississippi, Kentucky, Ohio, Indiana, Illinois, and parts of Pennsylvania and Virginia. These men planted their feet on this great territory and firmly held it. In war, as in peace, the doctrine of *uti possidetis* goes far in fixing titles.*

---

* Mr. Theodore Roosevelt, in his very able and instructive work, "The Winning of the West," has brought out the facts above referred to more fully than any previous author. I cheerfully acknowledge my indebtedness to him.

CHAPTER III.

THE COVENANTERS IN THE SOUTH.

Difference between grievances of Puritans and Covenanters—
Dependence of New England—Enforcement of Navigation
Act—Resistance thereto—Tumults—Closing the ports of
Boston—Charter revised—Sympathy and aid of other
Colonies for Boston—Love of Massachusetts for England—
Love of Cavaliers for England—Slow to break away from—
Covenanters hated England for her wrongs to them—
Were every-where active in opposition to England—
English influence in Southern Colonies—Episcopalians—
A majority of population in the South—That of Virginia,
New England, of all the Colonies—Covenanters in New
England—Number in all the Colonies—The most nu-
merous race—Number of Cavaliers—Covenanters in Penn-
sylvania, Virginia, Georgia and North and South Carolina—
Spread into all the new States of the South—Percentage of
foreign blood in the States—Tories numerous in the Revolution—Covenanters most numerous fighting race—They
settle in the South—" Puritans of the South "—Contrast
between Puritans and Covenanters—Massachusetts and
Virginia in the Revolutionary Army—Puritan warfare in
the South—Splendid record of Massachusetts in the Revolution.

To fully understand the mind and the spirit of
the people of the Colonies at and previous to the
Revolution, their antecedent histories must not be
overlooked. In this way only can their inner

7

motives be judged and their actions understood. Take the three leading peoples, the Puritans, the Cavaliers and the Covenanters, for illustration.

When the causes arose which led up to a clash of arms, the Puritans had been in New England nearly one hundred and fifty years. Whatever may have been their feeling toward the people in England, on their arrival in this country, they had been here long enough to outlive any bitterness they may at first have felt. Certainly they did not have to forget and forgive centuries of wrongs, nor did they cherish enmities which had been heaped up from generation to generation. In their new home for a long time they suffered no great oppressions inflicted by the mother country. The troubles which finally drove them and the people of the other Colonies into rebellion were in part merely wrongs in principle, rather than actual wrongs. These grievances, however, whether real, or merely menaced, were quite sufficient to justify before the tribunal of history the measures of resistance adopted by them, and it must be admitted that no people were ever more prompt in assuming their natural right to independence among the nations.

The dependence of New England on the mother country during all its colonial days down to a

period recently before the Revolution was more
nominal than real. In the exercise of power and
authority—in a word in all matters pertaining to
their own internal affairs and self-government—
they were nearly as independent and as free from
constraint in 1760 as in 1780. This statement
holds good as to the other Colonies also. The
people of New England were not until a late
period goaded on toward rebellion, and constantly
exasperated by unceasing and intolerable oppressions. They had not, therefore, been hoarding up
their wrath for a day of vengeance.

But a time was to come when the mailed hand
of England was to be laid with all its weight on
Massachusetts. The first great controversy grew
out of an attempt to more strictly enforce the
Navigation Act, which had been passed by Parliament to restrict the trade of the Colonies. This
act was partial, unjust, and oppressive. Its provi-
sions were often evaded by smuggling. When
this became known, application was made to the
Court for " Writs of Assistance," to enable the col-
lectors of ports to search for and seize smuggled
goods. James Otis, Jr., though Advocate-General,
refused to represent the Crown, resigned, and
appeared for the people, in opposition to the writs.
This was in February, 1761. The indignant elo-

quence of Otis, in behalf of popular rights, burst
forth in a flame of fire. The Crown triumphed,
but popular liberty that day had its birth in Massachusetts. John Adams, who was present, says:
"American independence was then and there
born." Then followed the Stamp Act, and after
its repeal, the tax on tea. At each new invasion
of their privileges, the people became bolder and
more defiant in their defense. With a daring,
not to say an audacity almost unparalleled, they
boarded the vessel containing the tea on which the
duty was to be paid, emptied it into the bay, and
then quietly returned to their homes as if nothing
had happened. Riots were frequent in the streets
of Boston. In one of these, three citizens were
killed by British soldiers. Excitement and patriotic feeling rose to a white heat. To punish these
turbulent friends of liberty, the port of Boston was
closed against all outgoing and incoming vessels.
Trade and commerce were to be cut off from the
insolent city. Its charter was revised so as to
take away its ancient rights and bring its government under the control of the Crown. But Boston
stood firm. The people yielded not one iota of the
principles for which they contended, though they
saw their commerce destroyed and poverty invading their homes. In the day of peril and

gloom, no people could have manifested a loftier spirit, a firmer purpose, or a more exalted patriotism. Their conduct was heroic.

While the people of Boston were enduring these trials with a sublime courage, the people of the Colonies were not indifferent spectators of their sufferings. The cause of Massachusetts was made the cause of all. On learning that the port of Boston was closed, Virginia, Maryland, and New York sent supplies for the relief of the city, with brave words of encouragement. Other Colonies did the same thing. Christopher Gadsden, of South Carolina, in sending a generous contribution, said: "Don't pay for an ounce of the d——d tea!"

After more than a century of peaceful existence and comparative independence, the people of Massachusetts suddenly saw themselves treated as aliens, as a conquered race, and their most cherished rights rudely assailed. And yet to the last, like dutiful children, they were reluctant to sever the tender ties of consanguinity. Their ideas were all English. They felt pride in English history and in English glory. Their ancestors had helped to make for England its proud position. Its history was a part of their heritage. England was their native land, their mother country. Many of their kindred were still there. The English were their fellow countrymen. The ties of blood bound the two together in a common sympathy. As children, they were slow to break away from their parent. When finally driven into a hostile conflict, there was as much of sorrow as of anger on their part.

It was subsequent to May, 1775, before John Adams uttered his first public word in favor of separation and independence.*

In the case of the Cavaliers of Virginia, the facts were even stronger in the same direction than with the Puritans. There was on their part an enthusiastic attachment for England. They were the petted children of royalty. They loved England and English institutions with all the ardor of grateful children. The English Church, too, they loved with deepest devotion. It was another bond to tie them to the mother country. They witnessed with sad hearts the estrangement gradually becoming more and more manifest between the King and the Colonies. They were slow to tear themselves away from royal sunshine and the splendor of royal greatness. Some never did so. Others, when they recognized that an inevitable conflict had come, one which could not be averted, smothered their traditional love for their mother

---

* Presbyterians and the Revolution, 77.

land, and threw themselves into the great struggle on the side of independence with all the ardor and impetuosity of their ancestors fighting under the fiery Prince Rupert. But mark, these were not the men who urged forward the Revolution in its inception. As we have seen, this had been the work of Patrick Henry and of his Covenanter associates. As late as August 1, 1775, Mr. Jefferson said: "I would rather be in dependence on Great Britain, properly limited, than on any nation on earth, or than on no nation."

In May, 1776, Washington said: "When I took command of this army (June, 1775), I abhorred the idea of independence."

These were patriotic Episcopalians, as true to the American cause as men could be, and yet reluctant to break away from the mother Church, and from the splendor of the British Crown. Long before this time, Patrick Henry, who was bound by no inherited and traditional ties, had exclaimed: "If we wish to be free, we must fight; I repeat, we must fight. . . . There is no retreat but in submission and slavery."

Turning to the Covenanters, we find a marked contrast between them and the other two races. They were not Englishmen, though the two peoples were originally of substantially the same Teutonic blood.   For centuries, the kingdoms of Scotland and England, and the people of the two kingdoms, had been enemies, always at war with each other, or with minds at all times ready for war.   They were practically alien enemies.   Scotland accepted the Reformation with singular unanimity, and adopted the Presbyterian form of Church government.   England also accepted the Reformation, but adopted Episcopacy, and made it the religion of the State.   In the course of time, the Covenanters were denied the right to exercise their own chosen religion according to their own forms.   Both in Scotland and Ireland, efforts were made by the Sovereigns of England, instigated by the Bishops, during a part of the seventeenth and most of the eighteenth centuries, to deprive them of their cherished faith, and to impose on them a worship they abhorred.   This was accompanied in Scotland by a century of heartless atrocities and persecutions, and in Ireland by broken faith and unfulfilled promises on the part of the government, by cruel injustice on the part of the Bishops, and by extortion on the part of the English landlords. At last, filled with hatred of every thing English, and burning for revenge, these spirited and ill-treated Covenanters fled to the Colonies.

When the curtain began to rise on the great

drama of the Revolution, the outrages inflicted on these people were recent and fresh in their memories. It was not alone the wrongs borne by their ancestors one hundred and fifty years before which they remembered. True, they had these, as the Puritans also had them. But many and grievous were the cruelties the Covenanters themselves had endured. The memory of Claverhouse's victims, the slaughter of poor unarmed peasants at Both-well Bridge, the atrocities of the Highland soldiers, the cries of agony wrung from strong men by the rack, the boot, and the thumbscrew in the secret chambers of the Old Castle at Edinburgh, the crackling fire as it slowly enveloped the writhing victims chained to the stake—all these and a thousand more persecutions were well remembered. But ten times more vividly than these were recalled the recent wrongs, which many of those living had endured in Ireland, when they were evicted from their little homes by heartless landlords, when their schools were closed by order of the Bishops, when their ministers were silenced and deposed from their own churches, when they were forbidden to bury their dead, except according to Episcopal forms. All these and many more grievances were burned into the very souls of these men. The accumulated wrath of long, terrible years, stored up in their minds, was ready to burst forth into a flame. The Covenanters had come indeed to hate England and everything English with an intensity and a depth of bitterness seldom found among any people. They had longed for the day when they could repay England and the English Church and the English landlords for countless oppressions. The opportunity was now at hand. And everywhere throughout the Colonies, from Maine to Georgia, were scattered this determined English-hating people, ready and foremost in stirring up the strife and in demanding resistance and separation. The multiplied grievances of two centuries were now to be avenged. It is shown elsewhere that at the time, these men, so ready, so eager for resistance, were regarded by Tory and Episcopal writers as chiefly responsible for the War of Independence. But for their influence, it is doubtful whether a single Colony south of New Jersey could have been brought into the plan of resistance and in favor of separation. In Pennsylvania, they pushed the obstructing Quakers aside, and took the control of the Colony into their own hands. In Virginia, they overawed the aristocratic English-loving people of the Eastern Counties, and either insured co operation on their part, or the flight of those who still adhered to the royal cause.

In North Carolina, the spirit of the Mecklenburg Resolutions animated the majority of the people, in spite of the English influences at work. In South Carolina, notwithstanding there existed a considerable tory power, the Covenanter spirit (combined with that of the Huguenots), under the lead of Rutledge, Sumter, Gadsden, Moultrie, the Pinckneys, Pickens, Huger, and Tennant, placed that State alongside of the foremost Colonies in the great patriotic uprising.

It must be kept in mind that the original settlers in all the Colonies, excepting New York, New Jersey, and Delaware, and perhaps to some extent in Pennsylvania, were largely, and in most cases, almost exclusively English people. All the Colonies were settled before the advent of the Covenanters. The English, especially in all the Southern Colonies, were generally if not nearly universally of the established church, and many of them royalists. They favored, as a remedy, remonstrance, petitions, and delay. And but for the large Covenanter population in the Colonies, English influence in all probability would have prevailed in their councils, and the Revolution would have been postponed or defeated.

It is true that New England also like the Southern Colonies had been settled by people of English

birth, but they were not Episcopalians, but originally Calvinists in religion. Like the Covenanters, they had come to this country burning
with the memory of the persecutions they had endured in the mother country, but this was a long
time before. The generation that suffered had
passed away. They were not held to the mother
country by the sacred ties of a powerful and magnificent church, but repelled from it on that very
account. While many of their wrongs were not
recent, as with the Covenanters, they were in their
origin of such a fundamental character as to cut
them loose from any special love for England or
for the English people. When the Revolution
came on, there was nothing to hold the New England people back from giving it their cordial support. They were, therefore, animated in their
course by a love of liberty as well as by recent and
great injuries. The Covenanters had both motives
to spur them forward.

And yet New England alone could not have
carried the Revolution to a successful termination,
and would not alone have undertaken such a thing.
A majority of the population of the Colonies were
in the South. The five Southern Colonies contained
perhaps half of the English speaking race in
America. Virginia alone contained one-fifth of

the population, or about 550,000 souls. All the
Colonies together had only 2,750,000 inhabitants.*
Of that number more than 1,375,000 were in the
South. In 1790, when the first census was taken,
the population of the United States was a little
less than four millions. New England had at that
time 1,002,660 inhabitants, Virginia contained
747,610, while the State of New York had only
340,120. The increase from the Revolution to
that time was about thirty per cent. Supposing
the rate of increase to have been about the same in
the New England States that it was in the whole
country, it would have given them at the time of
the Revolution scarcely 750,000 inhabitants. Nor
were all the New England population of .750,000
of Puritan blood. There were some Quakers and
many Baptists. Rhode Island was a Baptist Colony. At an early day, as is elsewhere shown,
22,000 Covenanters settled in New England,† some
of them in 1718, and all of them in the first part
of that century. Douglas Campbell suggests that
there was probably a much greater number of this
stock in New England than is generally supposed.
They were numerous in New Hampshire, Ver-

---

* McMaster's Vol. I, 7, 8. This estimate is based on estimates made by DeBow, Vol. III, 404.

† Scotch-Irish Seeds in America, 277.

mont, and in Maine, as he points out, so much so
as to almost make the two first named Covenanter
States. The Covenanters who settled in New England fifty years before 1775 must have numbered
at the latter date 50,000 or 60,000. These, with
with the Quakers and the Baptists, probably made
the number, not of Puritan blood in New England,
fully 100,000, leaving the latter race only about
650,000, including slaves and indentured servants.

On the other hand, the Covenanters numbered
in all the Colonies at that time over 900,000, making them decidedly the most numerous people in
the country. When we consider the facts, this
should surprise no one. Between 1728 and 1750,
twelve thousand arrived annually in Philadelphia
alone.* Suppose they had only doubled in number
in these forty-seven years; then they would have
numbered in 1775 half a million. But the Covenanters who landed in Philadelphia were not the
only ones who came to the Colonies. They landed
at other ports as well: at New York, New Castle,
Baltimore; at Wilmington, Charleston, and Savannah. This immigration commenced about the
year 1700 and continued, with intermissions, until
the Revolution, a period of seventy-five years.

---

* Scotch-Irish Seeds in America, 276.

Sometimes the immigration was very active. "In the two years which followed the Antrim evictions," says Froude, "thirty thousand Protestants left Ulster." James Logan, President of the Proprietary Council of Pennsylvania, wrote, in 1729, that: "Last week not less than six ships arrived, and that every day two or three arrive also." Froude says: "That ships could not be found to carry the crowds that were eager to go." *

From the well-ascertained facts as to this remarkable immigration, the conclusion may be safely reached that, prior to 1775, not less than 500,000 people of the Covenanter race from Scotland and Ireland had settled in the Colonies. Putting the average length of time they had been here at thirty years, it can be safely assumed that they had increased at least eighty per cent during that time, making them number not less than 900,000 people in 1775.

It is clear that the Puritans, in 1775, could not have much exceeded 600,000, for in 1790 the whole population of New England was only a fraction over 1,000,000.

The Cavaliers in Virginia at that time could not have exceeded 400,000, if indeed they were nearly

---

* Scotch-Irish Seeds in America, 274.

so numerous, including their large number of slaves and white servants, since the whole population of the Colony in 1790 was only 747,610.* But suppose they numbered 450,000; it would only make them half as numerous as the Covenanters in the entire country. These estimates show that the Covenanters were, at the date of the Revolution, the most numerous of the three great subdivisions of the people in the country.

It has been computed that the Covenanters at that time amounted to one-third of the entire population of the country. This I think a very low estimate. This would give them 916,666 souls— about the same result reached by the previous process of calculation. The larger part of these were in the South, perhaps two-thirds, or more than 600,000. They therefore constituted nearly one-half of the entire population of the Southern Colonies and States. It will be evident, on a little reflection, that they were more numerous than any other single people. In New York, and especially in the western section, a large part of the population seems to have been of this stock. Delaware and New Jersey also had a large Covenanter population. In Pennsyluania, they were very numer-

_____

* Lecky says that they numbered 250,000 souls. England in the Eighteenth Century, Vol. III.

ous, being estimated at one-third of the population. Their influence upon passing events was greater than might have been expected even from their numbers. In 1775, in all the Southern States, they exercised considerable power. In North and South Carolina, their control was almost supreme, as it has been ever since. Ramsay, the historian of South Carolina, states that Ireland—that is, the Covenanter settlements—contributed most to the population of that State. Williamson says the same thing in reference to North Carolina.* It is admitted that Kentucky was peopled by them. It is equally clear that Tennessee, from the very first settlement has always been in the main under the direction of this people. Any one acquainted with the names of its early inhabitants, with the history of the old families, and their customs, and with that of the State, can have no doubt on this point. Indeed, the early settlers were almost entirely from the Covenanter population of Virginia and of North and South Carolina; as the population of Kentucky was from the Covenanters of Virginia and Pennsylvania.†

Georgia, also, was mainly settled by the Cov-

* Proceedings Scotch-Irish Congress, Vol. IV, 141.
† Id. 142.

8

enanter race. Oglethorpe's Colony failed in this
State in 1752. The New England Colony at Sunbury also failed.* Then came the Covenanters
"from the mountain and Piedmont regions of the
Carolinas and Virginia, and filled all Middle
Georgia." They have gone on from the day of
their arrival in Georgia, with that energy, intelligence, and persistence so peculiar to them, building up the State in its material resources, in intellectual achievements, in moral and religious works,
and in molding and shaping its institutions, until
to-day its pre-eminence among Southern States is
acknowledged by all the world.

And when Alabama, Mississippi, Louisiana, Florida, and Arkansas were opened for settlement, these
States were filled by the more numerous and dominant race from the older Southern States of Virginia, the Carolinas, Georgia, Tennessee, and Kentucky. To a large extent, indeed to a greater extent than from any other quarter, Missouri also
was settled from the same sources, it being a slave
State. Finally, Texas was at first built up almost
exclusively by a Southern population. Thus the

---

* For a particular account of this settlement and the achievements of the Covenanters in Georgia, I refer the reader to a
very able address by Patrick Calhoun before the Scotch-Irish
Congress, at Atlanta, in 1892, Vol. XIV, 136.

Covenanters, the more numerous stock at the date of the Revolution, were spread over the entire South. And to-day the blood of that people greatly predominates over any other in that section.

It is undeniably true according to both history and tradition that the early settlers of Tennessee and Kentucky, of West Virginia, and of all the upland regions of old Virginia and of North and South Carolina and Middle Georgia, were nearly all Presbyterians. If these were not Covenanters, let me ask of what stock they were?

Has the reader ever reflected as to the source from which the population of the Southern States, formed since the Revolution, came and from what stock? They did not come from the Northern States, except a few Germans, who settled in Virginia and Tennessee at an early day, and except a fairly large German population which settled in Texas and Missouri in later years. The Southern States never attracted immigrants either from the North or from abroad. The census of 1890 throws much light on this subject. The North Atlantic Division, consisting of the States of Maine, New Hampshire, Vermont, Massachusetts, Rhode Island, Connecticut, New York, New Jersey, and Pennsylvania, has 47.4 per cent of persons of foreign parentage. The South Atlantic Division, consisting of the

States of Delaware, Maryland, Virginia, West Virginia, North Carolina, South Carolina, Georgia, and Florida, has 6.02 per cent. The South Central Division, consisting of the States of Kentucky, Tennessee, Alabama, Mississippi, Louisiana, Texas, Arkansas, and Territory of Oklahoma, has a percentage of 7.50. The North Central Division, consisting of the Upper Mississippi Valley States, has 43.02 per cent. And the Western Division, consisting of the States and Territories west of Kansas and Nebraska, has a percentage of 48.67.

Let us take a few of the States for comparison: Massachusetts has 56.24 per cent of persons of foreign parentage; Connecticut, 50.32; Rhode Island, 58.02; New York, 56.65; Illinois, 49.06; Michigan, 54.72; Minnesota, 75.42; North Dakota, 78.98; California, 56.72. In the Southern States, Virginia has 2.63; North Carolina, 0.70; South Carolina, 1.53; Georgia, 1.78; Kentucky, 9.87; Tennessee, 3.02; Mississippi, 2.00; Texas, 15.00; Arkansas, 3.37.

These figures disclose a remarkable state of facts. They show that the only people of nearly a pure, original type and blood in the United States are in the Southern States, and that those approaching the nearest to the original type are found in the States where the Covenanters first settled in such great numbers, namely: in Virginia, West Virginia, North Carolina, South Carolina, Georgia, Tennessee, and Kentucky.

Returning to the question as to the stock from which a majority of the Southern people have descended, we must keep in mind that during the Revolution there was a large tory element in the Colonies. John Adams estimated that one-third of the people were of this class. Justin Winsor has estimated it at two-fifths.* These estimates at this day seem large, but we have no means of disproving or controverting them. The tories were certainly numerous in New York and Pennsylvania, and in all the Southern States. There was also a considerable number in the New England States. But of these tories the Covenanters formed no part. The only apparent exception to this statement were the Highlanders of North Carolina under Colonel Donald McDonald, who took up arms for the King in the Revolution. He and his followers had emigrated from Scotland thirty years before. There they had borne arms on the side of Charles Edward the Pretender, in the battle of Culloden. They were pardoned for their offense, on condition that they would leave

* Bryant's History, Vol. III, 455; Justin Winsor, History of America.

the country and bear true allegiance thenceforth
to the King. They were bound to the King by
this oath, as well as by gratitude for sparing their
lives. It is to their credit, rather than otherwise,
that they kept their oath, and manifested their
sense of obligation for the mercy, so uncommon in
that day, shown them. In addition to this the
Highlanders were not generally Covenanters;
many of them were Catholics. Aside from this
exception, if, in fact, it is one, there is no other
case, so far as I can find, in all the Colonies where
the Covenanters were untrue or unfaithful to the
great cause of American liberty. As I elsewhere
point out, Ramsay, the historian of South Carolina,* said that "the Irish" (that is the Covenanters) were almost to a man on the side of
Independence. In Pennsylvania this people was
united in favor of Independence, and contributed,
though only one-third of the population, a majority of the troops of the State to the Continental
army. The same was true, we are told, to a large
extent, of the States south of Pennsylvania.†

The influence this people exerted in the
Southern Colonies in the Revolution can be better
appreciated when we keep in mind how large a

---

* Fiske says that the Scotch merchants were loyalists.

† Campbell, Vol. II, 489, 490.

part of the population it formed. Deducting the tories and the Quakers, the Covenanters would appear to have been considerably more than one-half of the fighting population. And when we recall how anxious to take up arms they were, how united in an intense and common purpose to achieve Independence, we can realize the great work they did in the Revolution. We must further keep before us, in estimating their services, that they were the best educated race in the South; that they had great force of will and tenacity of purpose. As soldiers, they were as brave as any in the American army. And when we add to this the fact that they were urged forward by an ardent love of liberty, by a deathless devotion to their religion, and, as no other race was, by the maddening memories of recent wrongs which fired their whole beings, then their important service in securing Independence can be clearly seen.

We must keep in mind that the Quakers of Pennsylvania, Virginia and North Carolina, as before stated, would not bear arms. As we have seen many members of the established church adhered to the royal cause. The fact is undeniable that there was a large number of tories in the Colonies, and that they were for the most part

English. Many of them were pure, conscientious men who thought there was no justifiable cause for separation, and honestly preferred to remain under the rule of England. When hostilities commenced some of these quitted the Colonies and never returned, and some took up arms in the King's army, or refused to take part in the war. Some went to England, some to Canada, some to Nova Scotia, some to Bermuda, and others to the Spanish Territory of Florida.* In such cases, they lost caste, and were ever afterward held in the deepest detestation. The result was there was a large population who would not and did not fight for the Colonies. But the Covenanters, on the other hand, forming a majority of the patriots, were eager for the conflict.

When the tories and the Quakers were eliminated from the 1,350,000 souls in the Southern Colonies, only about 850,000 people were left from which to draw soldiers. Who were these 850,000 people? If previous estimates are correct, nearly or quite 600,000 of them were Covenanters. If much the larger number was not of this race, who were they? So far as I know, the Catholics of Maryland were true to the cause of Independence,

---

* McMaster, Vol. I, 108 to 120; Justin Winsor, History of America.

but they were not numerous. The Baptists also were every-where loyal to the Colonies, but their number was very limited. The Methodists in the country were also true and faithful. But that great church was then in its infancy. The Huguenots were as true to the American cause as the Covenanters, but their numbers were likewise small. The Germans who had settled in Virginia constituted but a small part of the population, so that not many fighting men could be drawn from them. Many of the Cavaliers fought for Independence; so also did a part of the English settlers outside of Virginia. But all these could not furnish as many soldiers as the Covenanters. In this view of the case, therefore, the fact must have been as stated by Douglas Campbell, that the Covenanters furnished to the Continental army a majority of its troops throughout the whole country south of Pennsylvania.*

From natural causes this people at an early day after their arrival in the Colonies seemed to set their face toward the South. This is partly explained by the fact that the Quakers of Pennsylvania, a majority of them having first landed there

* Campbell's Puritan, Vol. II, 490, 491, and notes.

9

on coming to this country, were unfriendly, and did all in their power to drive them southward or west of the Alleghanies. Many of them, from this cause, were forced by the hard terms of James Logan, the agent and secretary of the Proprietary Government, to seek homes in the western part of Pennsylvania. He spoke of them as "audacious and disorderly," and of their coming "where they were not wanted." The English authorities also persecuted and misrepresented them.*

It happened that many of them were driven out of the State. Numerous as were those who remained, a much larger number, perhaps, turned Southward toward Maryland, Virginia, the Carolinas, and Georgia. The South held out splendid attractions to them. Says McMaster on this subject: "The reason is obvious. The Southern Colonies had long before the Revolution become renowned as the seat of a lucrative agriculture. Nowhere could such tobacco be raised as was annually grown on the banks of the Rappahannock, the Potomac, and the James. The best rice on the English market came from the swamps of the Carolinas. Georgia was already famous for pitch, for indigo, for tar. New England, on the other

---

* Proceedings of Scotch-Irish Congress, Vol. III, 132.

hand, produced scarce enough corn and rye for the needs of her citizens." *

The climate in the South was mild and delightful. It was especially inviting to men who must necessarily be exposed to the weather wherever they might go until they could build little homes for themselves. The soil was fertile and generously yielded every thing needed to satisfy the wants of a plain people. So, at an early day, the Southern Colonies teemed with these hardy, industrious Covenanters. Wherever they went, in the South, they met others of their race, who, having landed at Southern ports, were working toward the interior of the country.

In the light of these facts, it is apparent why, in 1775, these Colonies, as we have seen, contained more than one-half of the population of the entire country, and why more than one-half of those friendly to the American cause were of Covenanter blood.

Climate and soil, as well as a vast interior country, open to settlement, gave promise of that peace, freedom, and security which, they were so earnestly seeking.

Oglethorpe's Colony failed in Georgia in 1752. The New England Colony at Sunbury also failed.

---

* History of People, U. S., Vol. I, 9.

Then came the Covenanters "from the mountain and Piedmont regions of the Carolinas and Virginia," and filled all Middle Georgia. This race has never failed. It has gone on from the day of its arrival, in Georgia, with that energy, intelligence, and persistence so peculiar to it, building up the State in its material resources, in intellectual achievements, in moral and religious works, and in molding and shaping its institutions, so that to-day its pre-eminence among Southern States is acknowledged by all the world.*

Douglas Campbell calls the Covenanters, or, as he designates them, the Scotch-Irish, "the Puritans of the South." It is not well to thus confound these two great peoples. Though the English and the Scotch people were originally largely of the same blood, they early became separated into two distinct people, each with peculiar characteristics of its own. It will be conceded that in certain respects there were some striking resemblances between them, especially between the early Puritans and the Covenanters. But the points of dissimilarity are more numerous and more marked than

---

* For a particular account of this settlement and the achievement of the Covenanters in Georgia, I refer the reader to an able address by Patrick Calhoun before the Scotch-Irish Congress at Atlanta, in 1892, Vol. VI, 136.

those of resemblance. In the stern austerity of
their religion, and in the somberness of their lives—
in a word, in the outward aspect of religious life,
they seemed to be very much alike. And yet the
traits which distinguished the one from the other
were clear, striking, and manifest. This became
the more evident, perhaps, after each had left its
native land, and had found a new home for itself
where its natural tendencies had room for development. The Puritan was an Englishman, with
English tastes, ideas, and habits. In common with
his countrymen, he believed in caste, in social distinctions, and in the inequality of men. In religion,
the Puritan believed with all the earnestness of his
strong nature that he was right, and, so believing, he
used the whole power of the Church and the State
in enforcing conformity to it. He permitted no
dissent. In his view there must be universal conformity, banishment, the whipping-post, or the
gibbet. The State was merely the ally of the
Church, useful only to enforce its decrees and dog-
mas. The latter was supreme over the minds, the
consciences, and the bodies of men. This was the
Church polity of Puritanism in Massachusetts.
The Puritans had not learned the lesson left to the
world by Charles V of Spain, who, after his abdi-
cation, spent the evening of his life in a vain at-

tempt to make two watches run alike. While a monarch, he had used all the vast power of his great kingdom, and all the refined cruelties of the Inquisition, trying to force his millions of subjects into absolute uniformity in religious belief; that is, to force all men to see, feel, and think, and, as it were, to run alike.

On the other hand, the Covenanter demanded in the Colonies total freedom of religion from the control of the State. He denied the authority of the magistrate, in any matter whatever, to interfere with conscience, religious beliefs, or religious practices. The religion of men should be, he insisted, as free as air, or the water of the hillside brook. As to Government, he was Democratic in all his ideas. In his long experience, he had seen the arrogance and the insolence of caste, he had felt its power and its enmity, and had come to hate it with all the strength of his soul. By reason of centuries of ill treatment and persecution, he hated England and every thing English as he hated no other country or people. Of all the people in the Colonies, he was perhaps the least affected by English ideas. It thus appears that the differences in thought, habits, and in religious practices between the Puritans and the Covenanters were wide, radical, and fundamental. So, to designate the

Covenanters, or the Scotch-Irish, by the name of Puritan, is to confound race history and race distinctions.

Before closing this chapter, I wish to call attention to the singular fact, that in the Revolution, Massachusetts furnished a larger number of men to the Continental army, in proportion to population, than any other Colony. It is remarkable, that she sent more troops into the army than the six Southern Colonies combined. The number of soldiers from Massachusetts was twice as large as that from Virginia, the leader of the Southern Colonies, though the population of the latter was nearly double that of the former.*   How can these remarkable facts be explained? Perhaps they are incapable at this late date of a satisfactory explanation. They seem to emphasize the fact that there was a much more powerful tory, or English, influence in the Southern Colonies than has generally been supposed. They, the tories, were not so numerous in New England as in the South. Perhaps the latter fact can be accounted for in part by the feeble condition of the English Church there. In all the Southern Colonies, however, which were principally settled at first by Englishmen, that

---

* University of Virginia Magazine, April, 1894, p. 308; Campbell's Puritan, Vol. II, 499.

church had a large following. If therefore, there were but few tories in New England, and if they were equal in number to the computation of John Adams, in the entire population of the country, then it would seem that in the Colonies south of New England they must have constituted nearly or quite one-half of the population. If this were the case, the people who were friendly to the American cause, and from whom soldiers could be enlisted for the army, were not nearly so numerous as indicated by the total population, This was unquestionably true in a large measure.

Perhaps another reason may have some force in it. The warfare conducted by the tories was largely of a predatory or guerrilla character. They preyed on Whig farms and settlements, and often on the helpless families of the patriots who were absent in the army. The outrages they committed were brutal and diabolical. Bitter as we sometimes suppose the Civil War of 1861–1865 to have been, it was, in comparison with the deadly strife of the Southern patriots and the tories, during the Revolution, as the gentleness of the dove to the fierceness of the vulture. This kind of warfare in the South, often made it necessary for the patriots to remain at home, to guard against the violent outbreaks of the tories. On this subject a recent historian says:

"Throughout that State (Georgia), and in South and North Carolina, there broke out a partisan warfare which had no parallel in any other part of the country. The loyal and the patriot parties were so nearly equally divided that each was confident of gaining the ascendency, and the bitterness of personal detestation intensified to cruelty the evils of ordinary war. A district of country remained loyal or patriotic so long as it was occupied by the troops of either one side or the other. Citizens served as militia when organized militia operations promised success; where success seemed hopeless, or protection was no longer afforded by the presence of regular troops, they fled to the swamps and the woods, and carried on a murderous and predatory warfare against their neighbors on the other side. . . . Nowhere else, except to a limited degree in Central New York, was the war so entirely a desperate civil war, where neighbor was arrayed in deadly hatred against neighbor, each holding his life at the price of sleepless vigilance, each knowing that the death of the other was his only security."*

---

* Bryant's Popular History United States, Vol. III, 613. See also King's Mountain and its Heroes.

In this way, tens of thousands of men, doubtless, who did not belong to the Continental army, and whose names did not appear on its rolls, took part in the war, either regularly or occasionally, from its inception to its close. It is doubtful whether a single private of the army of Sevier, Campbell and Shelby, who helped to win the signal victory of King's Mountain, and who fought in many other battles, can be found among the records of the war. Besides all this, from Western Pennsylvania to Florida, all along the frontiers of Pennsylvania, Virginia, Kentucky, North and South Carolina and Georgia, there were thousands of men who were kept constantly in the field, or in a state of preparation for defense, against the murderous warfare waged upon the infant settlements by the powerful Indian tribes of the South and West. And these men, who thus defended and saved the West and the South-west, though scarcely known to history, and perhaps not known at all on the rolls of the war, were as really and efficiently fighting the battles of the Revolution as were the soldiers under Washington.

So, it may well be doubted, whether, in all the Southern Colonies, where these conflicts with tories, British, and Indians were taking place, there was a single Covenanter or patriot who was not under arms a part of his time, though only a small percentage of the entire population would seem by the records to have been in the regular Continental army.

There was another reason why Massachusetts furnished more men to the Continental army than the Southern Colonies, and that was this: The storm of war first burst on that State. Suddenly Boston found her commerce destroyed, herself cut off from the sea, and her people besieged. The blow was as terrible as it was sudden. Quickly the people flew to arms. All New England rallied for the defense of Boston. The questions at issue involved not only the liberties of the people, but the privileges, the trade, and the commercial independence of Boston, and other coast towns. The seat of war was there. No such gloomy threatenings at that time hung over any other city or State, and never did exist in some of the Colonies. And so, until near the close of the war, New England was either the theater of active operations, or the enemy was not so far removed from her but that he might return to her territory again. Her citizens remained in the army, or in a state of preparation, all the time.

But, after all has been said that can be in explanation of the fact I have been considering, it

would be both unjust and uncandid not to acknowledge in the amplest terms the extraordinary zeal
and patriotism displayed 'by the people of Massachusetts during the Revolution. The period from
1761 to 1783 forms an illuminated chapter in her
history, written in letters of gold, and resplendent
in eloquence, courage, patriotism, and sacrifices.
How warm and bright when compared with the
dreariness of her "glacial period." "Her ice age"—
sterile, forbidding, unproductive, her history dotted
only with boulders and stunted growth—was gone.*
The "florescent period" had come.

---

* Charles Francis Adams's "Massachusetts; Its Historians
and Its History," 107.

CHAPTER IV.

THE COVENANTER AND THE CAVALIER.

Covenanters left out of consideration by writers and speakers—
The most numerous of the classes—Covenanter ideas pre-
vailed in Virginia—John Knox's declaration—Cavaliers
the ruling class in Virginia—Political and religious
opinions—Bloody penal Code—Religious disabilities—
Early inhabitants—Many densely ignorant—Sir William
Berkeley, Governor, on education—Education neglected—
Life among the upper classes—Feasting, frolicking,
drinking and gambling—Dissipation of the Clergy—
Cruelty to dissenters—Gloomy condition of the Colony—
The Covenanters appear in the Colony—They erect
Churches, start schools and spread westward—Patrick
Henry—His origin—Offers Resolutions in the House of
Burgesses denouncing Stamp Act—His speech on—The
Country electrified—Thomas Jefferson—Becomes a re-
former—The Presbytery of Hanover sends a petition to
the Legislature asking for freedom of speech—Then a
second, a third, a fourth, a fifth and a sixth—They at
last triumph—Bitterness of Mr. Jefferson toward the
Presbyterians—Was a freethinker.

Both writers and public speakers have long been
in the habit of dividing the men who have shaped
and molded the institutions of this country and
guided its destinies into two classes, the Puritans
and the Cavaliers, the one the representative of
Northern thought and civilization, and the other
of Southern. This leaves entirely out of con-

sideration the Covenanters, the most numerous and in many respects the greatest of the three races. At the time of the Revolution, as has been shown, the men of Covenanter blood were scattered every-where in the Colonies, and were especially numerous in all the region south of New York. It seems reasonably clear that when the Quakers lost their influence in Pennsylvania, by reason of their opposition to separation from Britain, the Covenanters became ascendant in the councils of that State, and thenceforward mainly controlled its destiny. In Virginia, it was not the thoughts and opinions of the Cavalier which mainly guided that Colony in the great crisis of 1775–6 and that were incorporated into the framework of her government. Cavalier thought, forms and principles, both in State and Church, largely passed away with the opening of the great Revolution. When Jefferson, Wythe, Mason, and others, were engaged in their important work of purging the constitution and the statutes of the State of the odious penalties and disabilities, in reference to religious worship, imposed on dissenters by the established church, they were undoing the work, hoary with age and wrong, of the Cavaliers, and substituting the ideas and principles of the Covenanters. The highest and the best thoughts of Virginia, the leading ideas incorporated into her government, as well as into the national government, were Covenanter rather than Cavalier thought.

It little matters by whom these thoughts and principles were put into organic form, whether by those of Covenanter blood, such as Patrick Henry and Edmond Randolph, whether by the half Covenanter Thomas Jefferson, or whether by James Madison, the disciple of John Witherspoon in his political education. Each and all of them had caught the spirit and the ideas of the great Covenanter, John Knox. Hear him as he spoke two hundred years before:

"The authority of kings and princes was originally derived from the people; that the former are not superior to the latter collectively considered; that if the rulers become tyrannical, or employ their power for the destruction of their subjects, they may be lawfully controlled, and proving incorrigible, may be deposed by the community as the superior power, and that tyrants may be judicially proceeded against even to a capital punishment."*

The ruling class in Virginia from its earliest settlement were the Cavaliers. Some of them

† The Scotch-Irish in America, Vol. I, 199.

were of the English nobility. Most of them
believed in an established church, which should
be supreme over the consciences and religious
conduct of men, with the king as its spiritual
head.

They had been the adherents of Charles I in his
struggles with Parliament and the people in 1640,
and when he was dethroned and beheaded many
of them fled to Virginia. Here the Episcopal
Church was established as the only lawful church,
and all men, whether members or not, or however
much they might detest it, were compelled to support it. More than this, all other religions were
forbidden. One of Patrick Henry's most thrilling
speeches was made in 1763, in defending three
Baptist preachers, who were indicted as "dis-
turbers of the peace" for preaching, as Henry
expressed it, "the gospel of the Son of God."

The penal code, probably adopted in England,
for the Colony of Virginia, and in force from the
earliest days, was, in reference to moral and religious duties, perhaps, the bloodiest ever enacted by
men. By it adultery was punishable by death, as
it was subsequently in Massachusetts and Connecticut. Under Dale's Code, absence from church
on Sunday, without a good excuse, was made a
capital offense. The penalty of death was pro-

vided for all those who should blaspheme the name of the Creator, and for those who refused obedience to their ministers, while persons who absented themselves from the church on week days were to serve in the galleys for six months.* These laws of Cavalier Virginia were never repealed nor modified until after the Revolution, though not always enforced.

The foregoing penalties were only a few of the many which enslaved men in Old Virginia. Hundreds, perhaps thousands, of persons—Quakers, Baptists, Moravians, and doubtless also many ungodly, unsanctified fellows who did not wish to row in the galleys for six months, for being absent from church on week days—were driven out of the Colony, and fled to North Carolina.

By 1750, persecution and narrowness had nearly run their dark course in Massachusetts and Connecticut, but in Virginia, on the contrary, the established church grew more intolerant as it grew stronger.† It was the stifling effect of the practice of the Cavalier Church on the young mind of Madison, which, in 1774, made him write to a

---

* Campbell's Puritan, Vol. II, 415. Citing Doyle's English Colonies in America, 115, 139.

† Parton's Life of Jefferson, 202.

10

Northern friend: "I want again to breathe your free air. . . . That diabolical, hell-conceived principle of persecution rages among some." . . . He then goes on to tell that there were at that time, "in a neighboring county, not less than five or six well-meaning men in close jail for publishing their religious sentiments." . . . These prisoners were Baptists. Nor is it much wonder that this ingenuous young man, on coming home from Princeton, fresh from the teachings of the grand old Covenanter, John Witherspoon, should have expressed the opinion that, "if the Church of England had been established and endowed in all the Colonies as it was in Virginia, the king would have had his way, and gradually reduced all America to subjection.*

For the first hundred years, the population of Virginia dwelt mostly in the low country, in the tide-water region, and on the banks of the Lower James, the Potomac, the York, and the Rappahannock. It consisted nearly exclusively of English gentlemen, English clergymen, some common mechanics and laborers, and large numbers of slaves and indented white servants. The aristocratic gentlemen who first settled the Colony were, as we have said, nearly all adherents of

* 1 Parton, 203.

the king. They constituted the ruling class, though
perhaps a minority of the people. Many of this
upper class were densely ignorant. The lower
orders were entirely without education.*   In 1671,
Sir William Berkeley, the Governor of the Colony, expressed, no doubt, the opinions of his
class, when he said: " I thank God there are
no free schools or printing, and I hope we shall
not have them these hundred years. For learning
has brought heresy and disobedience and sects
into the world, and printing has divulged them.
God keep us from both."

It would be very hard for the greatest thinker of
the day to say so much in favor of education, in so
few words, as was done by this Cavalier in the
words just quoted, though he meant them quite
otherwise.   With Cavalier ascendency and rule,
education, except with the higher classes, was neglected. It was thought important by many only
to educate the eldest son, who was to inherit the
estate, sit with the justices, and represent his
county in the House of Deputies.   He was sent to
William and Mary, an institution under the patron-
age and control of the Cavaliers.   All persons who
were destined for the church and bar were sent to
this college, but the great body of the people, in-

---

* Lecky's England in theEighteenth Century, Vol. III.

cluding a large number of the first families, grew up in ignorance. In the upper classes, life was spent, to a large extent, in drinking and feasting, in fox-hunting and horse-racing, in visiting and playing cards, and in attending balls, where the stately minuette was danced by the grave seniors and the jig by the young and volatile.

The clergymen had fallen into such habits as to become, as Bishop Meade, of the establishment expressed it, "the laughing stock of the Colony." A few were good and learned men, and did their duty faithfully, among them Bishop Meade himself. Says a pungent writer: "The greater number lived as idle hangers on of the wealthier houses, assisting their fellow idlers, the planters, to kill time and run through their estates.* . . Sometimes the clergyman was the president of the jockey club, and personally assisted in the details of the race course. It was common for them to follow in the chase; they figured as the patrons of balls, and were rather noted for their skill at cards.* But the great failing with the clergymen was their drunkenness, which helped even in that age and in that Colony of indulgence and excess, to bring reproach on the church and on religion." †

---

* Parton's Jefferson, Vol. I, 56.   † Id., 202.

Bishop Meade bore unequivocal testimony to this fact.

How cruel the Cavalier laws were against all who did not conform to the faith and the ritual of the church, and how dissenters were driven out of the Colony to avoid the dreadful penalties imposed on them has been shown. Says a writer: " At the time when the Yankee magistrates were hanging witches and whipping Quakers, Virginia justices of the peace were putting Quakers in the pillory for keeping their hats on in church, and were appointing jurors of women to examine for witch-marks on the bodies of old women." * John Burk, a historian of Virginia, intimates that a woman was burned to death in Princess Ann County for witch-craft, and adds that in all probability the case was not solitary.†

The condition of things in Virginia before the Revolution was indeed gloomy and almost hopeless. All freedom of speech, of conscience, of mind, soul and body was fettered and tied up, as with manacles, by the laws and the religion of the aristocratic Cavaliers. All growth was such as came only in spite of repression. Population increased because the climate and the soil were the most inviting perhaps on the continent. No colony

* Parton's Jefferson, Vol. I, 000.   † Id. 202.

had so many natural advantages. Her resources were prodigious. The cultivation of tobacco, like that of cotton at a later day in the South, was supposed to lead to speedy fortune. Thousands hurried over from England to repair their broken estates by engaging in its culture. Baptists and Quakers came into the Colony notwithstanding the bloody laws existing against them. But the great source from which the population was enlarged, was the constant and never-ceasing stream of Covenanter immigration which commenced pouring into the Colony about 1732.

In the meantime bigotry and Cavalier incapacity rested like a nightmare on the Colony. The lower class of white men, ignorant and lazy, bordered on a state of barbarity.* How could they have been otherwise? Who had held out a helping hand to them? What elevating example had been set before them?

During the more than one hundred and sixty years of Colonial existence and Cavalier domination in Virginia, not a single great name appears in her history; not one in letters, in art, in science, in invention or in war. Not a single great deed or event marks this period. The only thing of interest to the historian was the revolt of Nathan-

---

* Lecky's England in the Eighteenth Century, Vol. III.

iel Bacon, in 1676, against the wrongs that the people endured at the hands of the Cavalier Governor, Sir William Berkeley. The attempt failed, because it was premature by a hundred years. Bacon died just as the rebellion was declining, and in that way escaped the fate reserved for him, while his adviser, William Drummond, a Covenanter, who had been the first Governor of North Carolina, was summarily hanged.

There is, however, a bright gleam of sunshine apparent above this gloom, lighting up that dark, dreary waste, but for which even the most faithful and obedient children of the church could not have endured the oppression, and that is, that the laws in reference to conformity and religious duties were not rigidly enforced. Their violation was often secretly winked at and passed over, or the Colony would have become a Golgotha. The Covenanters were allowed to stretch along the borders of the northern and western settlements, because they became a protection for the older settlements against the hostile Indians.

While the Cavaliers of the tide-water country were engaged, between 1700 and 1775, in raising and selling tobacco, in purchasing and trading in slaves, in hunting and horse-racing, and in all the amusements of that rude age, the serious and ear-

nest Covenanters, quietly passing over from Pennsylvania, where, as before stated, they were not
well received by the Quakers, into the rich and
beautiful valleys of Virginia, were spreading west-
wardly toward Wheeling, or ascending the slopes
of the Blue Ridge, and occupying all the fertile
highlands of that magnificent country on the east
side of the mountains. Finally they overleaped
the summit of the Alleghanies, spread over their
western slopes, and occupied the beautiful and
fertile country of South-west Virginia.

While the Cavaliers and the clergy in Old Virginia were living easy lives of indolence and luxury, the Covenanters were felling the forests,
building cabins and houses, sowing and reaping
with their own hands, and engaged in all the hard
vocations incident to a pioneer's life. They were
occupied in making a state. They were gather-
ing around their little homes all the comforts that
industry could supply on the frontier. Earnest
men they were. There was little mirth or levity
among them. They were strong in will and firm
in purpose; robust, brave, brawny, Sabbath-keep-
ing and God-fearing men. They had a great mission to fulfill. Freedom of worship, freedom of
thought, freedom of conscience were to be estab-

lished.   In the wilderness they were to plant and build up civilization.   The things which their fathers had struggled for, they sought: "A free State and a free conscience."   There was little frolicking among these grave people.   Serious cares and duties demanded their attention.   All, young and old, male and female, were as busy as the passing hours, or the flowing brook.

Soon the rude church edifice went up, then followed the log-cabin schoolhouse.   Of all the men in the community, the minister was the busiest, with preaching, teaching, visiting the sick, giving advice as to the affairs of the settlement, and at odd hours, caught from other duties, laboring on the farm.   He was the head man of the neighborhood, and his opinion was sought on all points.   Many of these plain people, and all of the preachers, were graduates from the universities of Europe.   They were great scholars for that day.   Not only were the churches and the schoolhouses to be erected, but seminaries, grammar schools and colleges were to be provided.   Thus, in 1747, the rude structure of Liberty Hall, since grown so famous and so great, arose in the wilderness.   Under the fostering care of the Presbytery of Hanover it grew until it became Washington College.

11

Liberty Hall! Significant and auspicious name! Truly it became a light set on a hill.

Into this region of Virginia came the Prestons, the Pattons, the Stuarts, the Breckinridges, the Campbells, the McDowells, the Alexanders, the Blairs, all of Covenanter stock. Among others of this wonderful Scotch people, there came John Henry, an educated man, and a nephew of the great Scotch historian, William Robertson. Patrick Henry was his son. The son learned a little Latin and something of English from his father, but he cared but little for books. He loved to hunt and fish and frolic, and was indolent and dreamy. Failing twice as a merchant, he read law six weeks and obtained a license. Soon he gained great notoriety by his celebrated speech in defense of the people, in the "Parsons case," as it is called. This was a suit, and a just one too, by the clergy for the tobacco allowed by law as their salaries, but under the whirlwind of Henry's eloquence the jury rendered an adverse verdict.

In 1765, Patrick Henry, this backwoodsman, dressed in home spun, took his seat the second time in the House of Burgesses. The coming Revolution was casting forward its dark shadows. Soon the news came that Parliament had passed the Stamp Act, taxing the Colonies. Every reflecting mind saw that to quietly submit was to become enslaved. The Colonies were agitated from one end of the country to the other. No one knew better than Henry that taxation without representation was contrary to the natural rights of men—was in fact tyranny. He had learned this from his race long before he saw a law book. No people in the world understood the laws of natural right so well at that time as the Covenanters. They had, in their hard experience, been studying and asserting them for more than two centuries. It was the violation of these laws that caused the presence of that long stream of stern Covenanters, constantly passing up the valleys of Virginia, moving westward, seeking homes, hunting out a place where they could have a "free church."

Henry waited for some one of the old members to move in the matter of the Stamp Act. They held back. The session was about to close. Burning with the fire of his own patriotic thoughts, he tore a blank leaf from a law book, and hurriedly wrote and offered in the House four resolutions, containing the germ of all that has been or can be said on the subject. These resolutions asserted, in their inner meaning, the right of the people to govern and to tax themselves. This

·was the key note to the Revolution, and the real
meaning of the Declaration of Independence. It
was the undertone and the interpretation of John
Knox's propositions, and of his answer to Queen
Mary. No new doctrine to the Covenanters. But
it startled, as from a dream, the old Cavaliers of
Virginia. The debate that followed was fiery, and
as Mr. Jefferson said, "most bloody." The old
leaders, Wythe, Pendleton, Bland and Peyton
Randolph, strove to defeat the resolutions. But
nothing could resist the wild tempest-like eloquence of Henry, "the forest-born Demosthenes,"
as Byron called him. As that awkward body
warmed and lifted itself up, it was transformed
by its own inward spirit into one of commanding
grandeur and majesty. That halting, stammering
voice rose and swelled until it now sounded like a
tempest, now it was like the noise of the storm
bowing the woods and the forests before it.
Finally, rising in the brilliant sweep of his oratory
to a climax, and stirred by his own great spirit, he
exclaimed in tones that thrilled every hearer:
"Caeser had his Brutus, Charles I had his Cromwell, and George III ——." "Treason!" shouted
the speaker; "treason! treason!!" echoed the ter-
rified loyalists springing to their feet. "And
George III may profit by their example," con-

tinued Henry. "If this be treason, make the most of it!"

The country was electrified by the audacious words of Henry. They rang and echoed through the land. The venerable citadel of royal and priestly bigotry was shattered to its foundation. A new force in government had been evoked—the ultimate power in all free government—the sovereignty of the people. In that hour New Virginia was born, and Old Virginia commenced passing away. While Henry was sounding the first notes of the coming Revolution in Virginia, James Otis and John and Samuel Adams were doing the same in Massachusetts. This was the first breach in the partition wall which separated the past—dark with the crimes of tyranny, intolerance and bigotry—from the future, already aglow with the promise of freedom and deliverance.

While this declaration of the rights of men was being proclaimed by Henry, there stood behind the bar of the House a modest young law student, cold and impassive, whose eager ears caught every word as they fell from the lips of the great orator. As he listens, he is transfixed and spellbound. This was young Thomas Jefferson, the friend of Henry then, and ever afterward. He was there watching his ungainly, plainly dressed friend, as he rose to make that speech which has given him immortality.

Eleven years after this time, this young law student of 1765 is in the Legislature of the State, himself now become immortal as the author of the Declaration of Independence. He is there as a Reformer, associated with two of the best and greatest men in Virginia, George Wythe and George Mason. He is there to lift and remove the burdens imposed on the minds, the consciences and the bodies of men by a century and a half of Cavalier misrule and priestly bigotry and bitterness. It is easy to see how the generous-minded Mason and the noble Wythe, who had emancipated their own slaves, should have been anxious to aid in removing from the statute book as dark a penal code as ever was devised by the haughtiest oppressors, and by the narrowest and the bitterest sectarians. But at first it is not so easy to understand how Jefferson, this half Randolph,* half Covenanter, this vestryman in the established church, should have been a reformer. He says he learned his lessons of freedom from Coke on Littleton; others say from the philosophers of France. But more likely he unconsciously im-

* Jefferson's mother was a Randolph. The Randolphs claimed descent from the Scottish Earls of Murray.—Parton.

bibed them from sources immediately around him
before he ever saw Coke, or he had read a
word of the writings of the great encyclopædists
of France, De Lambert, Diderot, Voltaire, Rous-
seau, Turgot and others. He was reared in the
country into which the Covenanters were pouring just as he was coming to manhood. He
was not ignorant of them, of their opinions, nor
of their history. He knew that the strong, brave,
educated people he was every-where meeting had
fled from Ireland to escape the very evils then to
be seen on every side in his own colony. He had
heard the red-hot words of Patrick Henry, in
his memorable speech, on that May day in 1765,
when in the House of Burgesses he proclaimed
the oracles and the creed of his fathers. That
the words had sunk deep into his mind there
is no doubt, so much so that in his old age
he always warmed with enthusiasm when referring to that great day. Out of his own experience and observation, it would seem, Mr. Jefferson would have learned, and with his generous,
noble nature, would certainly have realized the
crying need of reform, wide, radical and universal,
in his own State, especially as to liberty of conscience and freedom of worship. The sight of a
poor Baptist, or Quaker, in the pillory, or under-

going the agony of the whipping post, on account, not of crime, but of the neglect of some duty toward the church, ought to have been sufficient to keep him from both sleep and rest until the last dark spot on the State was forever washed out. Such a sight might have made the very stones cry out against the iniquity of such laws. We can realize how the picture must have affected a philanthropist like Mr. Jefferson. Even the sight of five or six Baptists in "close jail" for "publishing their religious sentiments" had made the gentle Madison sigh, in 1774, for the free air of another State.

But dull indeed Mr. Jefferson would have been if he had not perceived in his own mind the quickening spirit of the times, and felt the trembling of the approaching upheaval in every fiber of his being. A new force had entered the Colony. The sleepless Covenanters had planted their churches beyond the Blue Ridge, and had organized the Presbytery of Hanover, and so long as their remained a wrong under which they suffered, they would never cease to protest against it. This Presbytery, in 1774, sent its petition to the legislature, remonstrating against a bill devised to restrict religious rights. It asked "for that freedom in speaking and writing on religious subject

which is allowed by law to every member of the
British Empire in civil affairs;" a sentiment afterward, on motion of Patrick Henry, embodied in
the Virginia bill of rights.*

In October, 1776, there came another memorial
from Hanover Presbytery to the legislature, which
was considered in Committee of the whole House.
The result was, says Mr. Jefferson, that "after
desperate contests in that committee almost daily
from October 11th to December 5th, we prevailed
(only) so far as to repeal the laws which rendered
criminal the maintenance of any religious opinions,
and further to exempt dissenters from contributions to the support of the established church." *

What was the necessity of debating and considering for so long a time these simple proposition, presented by the sturdy Covenanters, dwelling beyond the mountains?   At this day all
Christendom receives them as true.   It was the
last death struggle of the old aristocracy in church
and state to hold on to its ancient power.

Scarcely had the echoes of the debate over these
propositions died away, when this same Hanover
Presbytery, from its session near Liberty Hall, in
1777, sent a third memorial to the legislature.
Then followed a fourth, then a fifth, and finally

---

* Scotch-Irish in America, Vol. II, 237.

a sixth. In 1785, there followed the " Covenanter Memorial," protesting against the incorporation of the Episcopal Church, and the act, " providing for the support of religion by taxation." The true and the whole doctrine in reference to the relation of religion and the state is contained in these words. Said Rev. William Graham in this memorial :

" The end of civil government is security to the temporal liberty and property of mankind, and to protect them in the free exercise of religion. . . Religion is altogether personal, and the right of exercising it inalienable; and it is not, can not, and ought not to be resigned to the will of the society at large, and much less to the legislature, which derives its authority wholly from the consent of the people."

Here was sounded the key-note to the whole question. And at Bethel Church, far over in the valley of Virginia, the Covenanters again came together, as they did at Gray Friars Church, in 1638, and ten thousand names were appended to this second league and covenant. And so at last, but not till 1786, after ten years' fight, the doctrines of the new covenant—of these backwoods Covenanters—were incorporated into the laws of Virginia, and the "act for establishing religious liberty," became a law.

How deeply rooted in the soil the old system had been, and how tenaciously its friends clung to it, may be inferred by the length of time it took to eradicate it. Jefferson and his co-workers, strong and great as they were, could not have succeeded when they did, long as it was after the Revolution, if it had not been for the votes, the encouragement and the moral power and force of the Covenanters. Says Campbell: "In the end, the work" (the reform) "was carried through by the energetic efforts of the dissenters, who formed a majority of the population, the Scotch-Irish Presbyterians being the leading element."*

A singular inconsistency in Mr. Jefferson is the extreme bitterness he manifests in his writings against the Presbyterians, i. e., "the Covenanters." In this great struggle, they were his strongest, his most advanced support. Without their aid, even after his long fight, he would have utterly failed to remove the shackles put on the minds, conconsciences and bodies of men, by the very church in which he was a vestryman. It was his efforts in this great reform perhaps, more than any single act of his life which gave him his reputation for

---

* Campbell, Vol. II, 492.

liberality. And yet he wrote of those who gave
him his chief support, if not his first hint on the
subject, as a bitter and narrow religious zealot
might have done of some opposing sect, and not
with the charity and broad-mindedness expected
of a great philosopher and philanthropist. He
knew how great the work of the Covenanters had
been in the Colonies in preparing the minds of the
people for the Revolution, and how conspicuous
and splendid had been their record in sustaining it
with patriotic ardor, and in helping to carry it
forward to a triumphant conclusion. He must
have realized that without their co-operation his
great "Declaration" could not have been made
good by arms before the nations of the world, and
that in that event his own name would have gone
down in history as that of a traitor. He knew of
the intelligence of the Covenanters and of their
great value as citizens. He knew their sturdy
virtues, the purity of their lives, their respect for
law, and their reverence for all things sacred. He
knew they were the best educated, and the most
sober and industrious people of Virginia, and that
their influence was always on the side of law and
good government. Yet, in his later years, he
wrote of them, as Presbyterians, as he might have
done of almost worthless outcasts, and with a

bitterness and a narrowness out of keeping with
his advanced age and his exalted standing. This
may be accounted for in part, when it is kept in
mind that he became what is known as a .free-
thinker. in religion, though he probably remained
a verstryman in the established church as long as
he lived.*

---

* In 1887, Mr. Jefferson wrote to Peter Carr as follows : " Fix
Reason firmly in her seat, and call to her tribunal every fact,
every opinion. Question with boldness even the existence of
a God ; because, if there be one, he must more approve
of the homage of reason than of blindfolded fear. You will
naturally examine first the religion of your own country.
Read the Bible then as you would Livy or Tacitus. For example, in the Book of Joshua we are told that the sun stood
still for several hours. Were we to read that fact in Livy or
Tacitus we should class it with their showers of blood, speaking statues, beasts, etc. But it is said that the writer of that
book was inspired. Examine, therefore, candidly, what evi-
dence there is of his having been inspired. The pretension
is entitled to your inquiry because millions believe it. On the
other hand, you are astronomer enough to know how contrary it is to the law of nature. You will next read the New
Testament. It is the history of a personage called Jesus.
Keep in your eye the opposite pretensions: (1) Of those who
say he was begotten by God, born of a virgin, suspended and
reversed the laws of nature at will and ascended bodily into
heaven, and (2) of those who say he was a man of illegitimate
birth, of a benevolent heart, enthusiastic mind, who set out
with pretensions to divinity,· ended in believing them, and

was punished capitally for sedition, by being gibbeted, according to the Roman law, which punished the first commission of that offense by whipping, the second by exile, or death *in furca*. . . . Do not be frightened from this inquiry by any fear of its consequences. If it ends in belief that there is no God, you will find incitements to virtue in the comfort and the pleasure you will find in its exercise, and the love of others which it will procure you. If you find reason to believe that there is a God, a consciousness that you are acting under his eye and he approves of you, will be a vast additional incitement; if that Jesus was also a· God, you will be comforted by a belief of his aid and love. Your own reason is the only oracle given you by heaven. And you are answerable, not for the rightness, but the uprightness of the decision." Parton's Life of Jefferson, 335.

CHAPTER V.

THE COVENANTER AND THE CAVALIER—CONTINUED.

Love of Church and loyalty to King in Virginia—Love of liberty—Nathaniel Bacon—Mr. Burke on love of liberty in
the South—Landed estates in Virginia—Tobacco used as
money—Indentured servants—Splendid hospitality—Covenanter element introduced—Covenanters superior to Cavaliers—Patrick Calhoun on the Covenanters—Education
among the Covenanters in the Colonies, in Ireland—In
North Carolina, in South Carolina and in Georgia—Covenanters in New Hampshire—Roosevelt on early inhabitants of Tennessee and Kentucky—Covenanters on the
Holston—Covenanters not paupers—Why education de-
clined with Southern Covenanters—Covenanter influence
in forming the institutions of the South—Little known of
the Covenanters—The reason of this—Henry Watterson
on the Covenanters—They made the Southern States—
Their monuments—Great names among them—Their influence in making the West—Covenanter ideas and characteristics in Southern society—Preach the same faith
their fathers did—Southern women—High moral and religious standard in the South.

Notwithstanding the paucity of great names in
the history of Virginia previous to the appearance
of the master minds of the Revolutionary epoch,
there certainly arose then above the horizon splendid lights of marvelous brilliancy: Washington,
Henry, Jefferson, Madison and others. How grand

in outline! How majestic in intellect! These
were the products of the storm of the Revolution.
They were the children of the new era in human
progress. But for it, they would have died and
been forgotten, as their ancestors had died and
had passed forever from the memory of man.
Great events make great men. They quicken the
human intellect and stir its powers to unwonted
intensity. The Revolution aroused the fires of
genius from their slumbers, and they leaped forth
with a splendor rarely paralleled in history. It
gave the world the peerless Washington; it gave
it Patrick Henry with his tongue of flame. The
darkness which had overshadowed old Colonial
Virginia was followed by a display of genius of
surpassing brightness.

I would not underestimate the ante-Revolution-
ary people of Virginia. They were a brave, a
noble and an honorable race of men, though
haughty and imperious. The two dominating, all-
controlling passions of their lives were love of the
church and devotion to their king. They struggled long to save their church unshorn of its
power. In none of the Colonies was loyalty so
deeply rooted as in Virginia. All the sufferings
of the early settlers were only evidences of their
love for their king. Intense as this feeling was

in the days of Charles I, it lost none of its force
in subsequent reigns.   It cost the old aristocracy
of Virginia many a bitter pang to give up their
sovereign.   It is almost impossible for this generation to realize the depth of devotion felt for the
mother country.   Its history, its traditions, its
glory were a part of their own inherited possessions.   Affectionate, even enthusiastic love of the
royal house was a sentiment which had descended
from father to son.   It was interwoven with their
very beings.   To sever this bond of attachment
and to break away from these hallowed recollec-
tions was indeed a severe trial.

The Cavaliers were a proud-spirited race.   They
were acutely sensitive and jealous of their privileges.   They would submit to no wrong, either as
private individuals or as citizens of the Commonwealth.   Enthusiastically and warmly devoted to
their rulers and to the mother land as they were,
they loved liberty and their chartered rights just
as much.   They were far from being abject slaves.
Nathaniel Bacon, the leader of the first rebellion
in the Colony, was an educated gentleman, a man
of wealth and high social distinction, a member of
Governor Berkeley's council.   Yet he drew his
sword against kingly authority in defense of the
     12

rights "accorded in the royal charter." * The
spirit of freemen still animated the minds of the
Cavaliers. In the Revolution, in the supreme
hour of peril, after years of remonstrance, petition
and humble supplication, sad as was the alternative, many of them, perhaps a majority, turned
away from the memories and the splendid records
of the past and bore arms for their country.
When the great conflict was at hand, and it became evident that a stand must be taken, they
threw away their cherished and most sacred sentiments and nobly sustained the cause of independence.

Mr. Burke is quoted by Philip Alexander Bruce,
in his recent history of Virginia in the seventeenth century, as attributing the ardent love of
liberty during the Revolutionary era, in the Southern Colonies, to the institution of slavery. The
fact is undeniable that no people in any country,
or in any age of the world, have possessed the
spirit of liberty in a higher degree than the people of the Southern States. Most of this was due,
and especially so in the Revolutionary epoch, to
the spirit of the Covenanters. There seems, how-

* Address of Rev. Alexander White before Scotch-Irish Congress, Vol. IV, 122.

ever, to be much truth in Mr. Burke's conclusion. He said:

"There is a circumstance attending these Southern Colonies which makes the spirit of liberty still more high and haughty than in those to the northward. It is that in Virginia and the Carolinas, they have a vast multitude of slaves. Where this is the case, in any part of the world, those who are free are by far the most proud and jealous of their freedom. Freedom is to them, not only an enjoyment, but a kind of rank and privilege. Not seeing there that freedom, as in countries where it is a common blessing, and as broad and general as the air, may be united with much abject toil, with great misery, with all the exterior of servitude, liberty looks among them like something that is more noble and liberal. I do not mean to commend the superior morality of this sentiment, which has at least as much pride as virtue in it; but I can not alter the nature of man. The fact is so; and these people of the Southern Colonies are much more strongly, and with a higher and more stubborn spirit attached to liberty, than those to the northward. Such were all the ancient commonwealths; such were our Gothic ancestors; such, in our days, were the Poles, and such will be all masters of slaves who are not slaves themselves. In such a people, the haughtiness of domination combines with the spirit of freedom, fortifies it, and renders it invincible."

The landed estates of the wealthy in Old Virginia, were of immense size. Recent investigations have shown that their average size was about five thousand acres. Some estates amounted to twenty-five thousand acres. The chief industry in those days, indeed almost the only one, was the cultivation of tobacco. This formed almost the sole article of export. This was exchanged in European markets for such articles of necessity or luxury as the planters needed. These included nearly every thing. There was no paper money and but little coin in the early days. The wealthiest men seldom had more than thirty shillings in coin. Tobacco was the medium of exchange. It passed at a fixed value per pound and was a legal tender for all debts. In it, at a price fixed by law, tithes, taxes and debts were paid.

These vast landed estates required large numbers of laborers. Free white labor could not be had, and probably was not desired. Large numbers of indented, or indentured servants were used for this purpose, as well as African slaves. These indentured servants were white men, who were sold into slavery for a term of years, because of crimes, or political offenses. For the time being they were as absolute slaves as the African negroes.

On these great estates reigned a splendid and generous hospitality, after the style of Old England. Exchanges of visits were constantly taking place between tha wealthy planters. On every plantation the door of "the great house" stood wide open to all persons of "good conditions" who chose to enter. Feasting and the pleasures of entertaining formed a large part of the life of the old Virginian. It was in this school that the sons of the Cavalier Colony earned their reputation for the most profuse and elegant hospitality known on this continent, which distinction was still sustained by their descendants, as long as slavery lasted, with scarcely diminished honor.

But it must be kept in mind that with the inception of the revolutionary movement, the new and powerful Covenanter element, shown in the preceding chapter, was introduced into the councils of the Commonwealth of Virginia. To this a large part of the glory of the state must be attributed. How to apportion this glory between the two peoples with any thing approximating exactness and justice, it is impossible to determine. It is sufficient to say that many distinguished, and some great names, belong to each class.

Since the Revolution the old Cavalier stock of Virginia has borne a most honorable and conspicuous part in the history of this country. It were needless to attempt to enumerate their many noble qualities, or to set forth their achievements, in statesmanship and in arms, since they are known of all men. Virginia is no longer a Cavalier State, but a happy blending of the blood of both the Cavalier and the Covenanter—of the best qualities of both united in one.

But comparing the old races as they were prior to the Revolution, and counting also their faults and defects, I do not hesitate to say that, in the essentials that constitute a mighty people, of the two the Covenanters were decidedly the superior. This will be more manifest as I point out briefly some of the distinguishing characteristics of the Covenanters.

In courage, persistency, fortitude, firmness, natural capacity, purity of life, and in high moral and religious principle, no people ever surpassed them. Their industry and thrift were proverbial. In love of liberty, and in quickness to discern and resist every approach of oppression and wrong, an experience of centuries, had made them the foremost people in the world. Their long and bitter trials in struggling for freedom of conscience had given them the true 'idea of religious toleration, as it exists to-day in every State in the Union, and as it is fixed in the constitution of every commonwealth. They required for themselves the fullest liberty in religious matters, and both in Ireland and in the Colonies generously conceded the same to all other sects. They did not demand that their church should be made *the* church, but that it should be equal with all others. They did not seek to impose restrictions on other religions, nor to gain peculiar privileges for their own. Though their fathers, at an early day, in Scotland, had persecuted men for opinion's sake,* a century and a half of suffering, of trial, of development, had lifted them up to an elevation of larger vision and of more charitable thought. And except for the voice, the influence and the votes of the Covenanters in Virginia, it may be safely affirmed that Mr. Jefferson and his associates could not have removed the deeply-rooted and strongly-entrenched Cavalier restrictions on a free religion in that State.

On these points the remarks of Mr. Patrick Calhoun, in his address before the Scotch-Irish Congress, in Atlanta, in 1892, are so pertinent that I venture to quote a couple of paragraphs :

---

* Lecky and other writers say that at an early day they were narrow and bitter.

" In what striking contrast was the advent of
the hardy pioneers who had left home and fireside,
for conscience sake, to seek liberty and freedom in
the wilderness of America. They wrote their
history with the rifle and the ax, the sword and
the plow. There was no herald of their coming,
save the splash of the pole as they pushed the
rude ferry-boat across the upper waters of the
Savannah, or the crack of the whip as they urged
their tired. beasts, drawing primitive wagons over
rough mountain roads. The record of their coming was lost as the ripples of the river sunk back
into its current, or the echoes of the mountain
died away in its silence. We know neither the
day, nor the month, nor the year when thousands
came. But the fact that they had come was attested by the falling of the trees. Cabins rose and
fruitful farms appeared where forests grew and
Indians roamed. And not far off the church, the
house at once of worship and education." . . .

"From the time when the Scots left the north
of Ireland to the period when the Ulster plantation was settled, in 1609, Scotland was one constant theater of war. The sterility of the country, the clannish life its people led, the constant
dangers to which they were exposed, the frugal
manner in which their surroundings compelled

them to live—all contributed to produce a brave
and hardy race. Alone frequently in the mountains, forced to rely purely upon their own powers, there was developed in a marked degree not
only physical courage, but that high moral courage and reliance which have so distinguished the
race, and enabled it under all circumstances to
stand so unswervingly for what it believed to be
right, and made it ready to sacrifice home, family,
hope of emolument, life itself, for the dictates of
conscience. Love of individual liberty, devotion
to home and family ties, the habit of reflection,
promptness and decision in action, deep religious
convictions, belief in self-government, and a readi-
ness to resist the central power in the interest of
the clan, were characteristics naturally growing
out of the environment of the Scots. They were
frequently overrun by stronger and more numerous forces, but they were never conquered. The
sturdiness, endurance and persistency of the race
enabled them to surmount every form of conquest
and oppression. The moment the pressure of superior power was removed, the rebound occurred,
and Scotland was again in arms fighting for her
rights. The indomitable courage of the Scot was
invincible. Their natural characteristics could not

13

be destroyed, even by merger with other races. The Dane, the Saxon and the Norman settled in Scotland, and their blood is liberally intermingled in the veins of the Scotch, but the virility of the Scotch blood has preserved its distinctive national traits. Not even centuries of union with England could destroy these. The Scots were stronger for their life in Scotland, better for the blood of the Pict, the Dane, the Saxon and the Norman. When they returned to the north of Ireland, they found nothing there to weaken or enervate, but much to temper and to strengthen. Transplanted to the wilderness of America, their environment was as well calculated to develope their courage, independence and sturdiness of character as the lives their ancestors had led in Scotland. They were the pioneers of civilization and stood for more than half a century as the guards and protection of the Colonists nearer the coast. To the hardship of the frontier and the wilderness was added the daily fear of Indian attacks. And then the war school of the Revolution! Is it a wonder that with the numbers the Scotch and Irish had contributed to the population of the Colonies—is it a wonder that with the character stamped by the action of centuries upon their lives, they should have played an important part in that great

historical drama? Is it a wonder that* Froude
gives to them the credit of having won independence for America, and goes so far as to suggest
that even Bunker Hill was borrowed from Ireland?
It was these people and their descendants who,
pouring into Middle and Upper Georgia, gave direction to its civilization." * . . .

In education, the Covenanters were superior to
any other people or sect which came to the Colonies. If they were equaled by any, it was only by
the higher class of the first Puritan settlers. As
a whole they were far better educated than the
Puritans. "After the death of the first settlers,"
Campbell says, "there was a marked decline
(among the Puritans), not only in education, but
in all manifestations of a liberal spirit in every
direction." † Prof. Jameson said: "Puritanism
(had) gone to seed, grown narrow and harsh and
petty." ‡

At the time the Covenanters left Scotland for
Ireland, the state of education was higher and
more universal in that country than in England.
The Covenanters did not deteriorate in Ireland in

---

* Proceedings Scotch-Irish Congress, Vol. VI, 136.

† Campbell, Vol. II, 494.

‡ The History of Historical Writing in America, by J.
Franklin Jameson, Ph.D., 21, quoted by Campbell.

this respect, but remained a more thoroughly edu-cated people than the English who were planted there at the same time. When they reached the Colonies, as I have already shown, their first care and thought, next after their religion, were to provide for the education of the rising generation.

Douglas Campbell says of the Covenanters: "Nor were they children of ignorance. Although their schools had been closed by law, they had found means of private instruction in the common branches, while those desiring a higher education—and they were very numerous—had made their way to the Presbyterian Universities of Edinburgh and Glasgow. When they came to America these Scotch-Irishmen were not only among the most industrious and virtuous, but they were, as a whole, like the early settlers of New England, probably the best educated of the English speaking race." *

Again, the same author says: "In the fields of education the debt of America to these immigrants" (Covenanters) "can hardly be exaggerated. Not only did they give life and character to Princeton College, and found the institution now known as the College of Washington and Lee,

* Campbell, Vol. II, 479, 480.

in Virginia, but they gave her free school system to New Jersey and Kentucky, and for nearly a century before the Revolution they conducted most of the classical schools south of the province of New York. It was in these schools that the fathers of the Revolution in the South, almost without exception, received their education.*

Along this same line, a recent writer says of the Covenanters of North Carolina :

"From the arrival of the immigrants" (the Scotch-Irish, in 1706) "dates the establishment of schools throughout the State. It is to the Presbyterian Church that North Carolina owes the establishment of her first classical schools, and during the second half of the eighteenth century the history of education in this State is inseparably connected with that of this denomination."

. . . "Almost invariably," says Foote (History of North Carolina) "as soon as a neighborhood was settled preparations were made for the preaching of the gospel by a regular stated pastor, and wherever a pastor was located, in that congregation, there was a classical school, as in Sugar Creek, Poplar Tent, Centre, Bethany, Buffalo, Thyatira, Grove, Wilmington, and the churches

* Campbell, Vol. II, 486.

occupied by Patillo in Orange and Granville Counties.*

Again, the same author says: "To the Scotch-Irish Presbyterians occupying Central and Piedmont Carolina is due the lasting honor of having established the first academies in the province, and it is said that it was through their influence that the clause providing for a university" (and for common schools) "was inserted in the initial constitution of the State."†

Again, he says: "The pioneer promoters of advanced educational work in North Carolina were Presbyterians."‡

The author enumerates by name fifteen classical and scientific schools, academies and colleges started by Covenanter ministers in that State in the eighteenth century, besides, doubtless, many more referred to in general terms. In fact, nearly the entire educational system in that State was in the hands of the Covenanters.

In South Carolina they were also active in the same cause. The celebrated school of Rev. Moses Waddell, at Willington, where so many great and distinguished men were educated, was the most

---

* History of Education in North Carolina, by Charles Lee Smith. Bureau of Education, Washington, 23.

† Id. 52.   ‡ Id. 109.

noted of all the Carolina schools. But there were others also. In Georgia they did a great work in the same cause, but not an exclusive one. In Virginia they spread education wherever they went. In Kentucky also at an early day they established schools and colleges. In Tennessee the first four colleges in the State were founded in the eighteenth century by Covenanters, or presided over by Covenanters.

In the historical society of New Hampshire there is an ancient parchment, dated 26th of March, "Anno Dom.," 1718, to which three hundred and nineteen names are appended. It is the petition of certain Covenanter, or Scotch-Irish, heads of families, "from Ulster, of the North of Ireland," addressed to Governor Shute, of Massachusetts, informing him of their desire "to transport ourselves" (themselves) "to his very excellent and renowned plantation," upon obtaining suitable encouragement. Of the three hundred and nineteen signers of this paper, all but thirteen, or ninety-six per cent, signed their own names in "fair and vigorous characters." *

The learned professor to whom I have referred, says in reference to this document: "It may well

---

* Prof. A. L. Perry's address before the Scotch-Irish Congress of 1890, Vol. II, of Proceedings, 107.

be questioned whether in any other part of the United Kingdom, at that time, one hundred and seventy-two years ago, in England or Wales, or Scotland, or Ireland, so large a proportion of promiscuous householders in the common walks of life, could have written their own names."*

On August 4, 1718, five ships came to anchor in Boston, having on board one hundred and twenty families of these adventurous Covenanters, numbering seven hundred and fifty persons, who had some months before sent that letter or parchment to Governor Shute, asking for permission to transport themselves to his "renowned plantation." A part of these daring people, probably fifty large families, settled in Worcester, Massachusetts.†

Some of this noble band of heroes, namely, sixteen families, settled at Londonderry, New Hampshire, and others in the Kennebec country, in Maine. The descendants of these pioneers in the course of a few years spread all over New England, and especially over New Hampshire and Maine. Indeed, these two states became largely Covenanter in population, especially the former.

As previously pointed out, the first public meet-

---

* Prof. A. L. Perry's address before the Scotch-Irish Congress of 1890, Vol. II, of Proceedings, 107.

† Id., 110, 111.

ing held in the Colonies, which set forth the precise essential principles of the Declaration of Independence, was held in the County of Worcester, Massachusetts, in 1773, where the fifty Covenanter families had settled more than a half-century before.* From this little hive came Matthew Thornton, a signer of the Declaration of Independence, and the renowned botanist, Professor Asa Gray.†

It is singular how events, remote from each other, in point of space and time, sometimes seem to duplicate each other. Thus, in 1776, the members of the Watauga Association, in Eastern Tennessee, most of whom were of the Covenanter stock, sent a memorial to the legislature of North Carolina, signed by one hundred and four persons, all of whom except two subscribed it with their own names.‡

Again, Mr. Roosevelt, in speaking of the early inhabitants of the large region in the South, first occupied mainly, and indeed, almost entirely, by men of Covenanter blood, says :

" In examining numerous original drafts of petitions and the like, signed by hundreds of the original

* Bryant's Popular History of the U, S., Vol. III, 472.
† Proceedings of Scotch-Irish Congress, Vol. II, 123.
‡ Ramsey's Annals of Tennessee, 137, 138.

settlers of Tennessee and Kentucky, I have been struck by the small proportion—not much over three or four per cent, at the outside—of men who made their mark, instead of signing."*

Fortunately we are not left in doubt either as to who these early settlers were, nor as to their moral standing and intellectual attainments. Mr. Roosevelt has resurrected a manuscript left by the Honorable David Campbell, a son of one of the Holston pioneer Covenanters, giving an account of the early settlers on the Holston in South-west Virginia. The settlers on the lower Holston, in Tennessee, were but an overflow of the people from the upper Holston. Campbell says:

"The first settlers on the Holston river were a remarkable race of men, for their intelligence, enterprise and hardy adventure, . . . were mostly descendants of Irish stock, and generally where they had any religious opinions were Presbyterians. A very large proportion were religious and many of them were members of the church."†

Nor did the Covenanters who sought homes in the Colonies belong to the lower or pauper class. Perhaps no people who ever emigrated to the

---

* " Winning of the West," Vol. I, 180.
† Id. 167.

Colonies, or to the States, as a whole, equaled them, and certainly none ever surpassed them, in material condition and circumstances. The colonists from Scotland who settled Ulster, under the charter of James I, of May 16, 1605, were *picked* men. James had agents for this very purpose. None but persons above exception were received. In one of the letters of Arthur Chichester, deputy of James for Ireland, he says: "The Scottish men came in better *port* (*i. e.*, manifest character), they are better accompanied and attended, than even the English settlers."* For many years, perhaps nearly a hundred, before the great emigration to America commenced, they lived in comparative peace in Ireland, and were very prosperous. Many of those who settled in the Colonies were wealthy. Campbell says: "In the first place, it should be noticed that they were not socially poor peasants, such as Ireland has contributed to America in later days. Among them were wealthy yeomen, and in their ranks were the most intelligent of Irish manufacturers." †

When the Covenanters landed in the Colonies they were comparatively independent in the mat-

---

* Proceedings of Scotch-Irish Congress, Address of Rev. Dr. McIntosh, Vol. II, 93, 94; Froude, 393.

† Campbell, Vol. II, 479, 480.

ter of property. Many facts might be given to sustain this statement.* Within my own observation, I know that the early settlers of Tennessee, who were largely of this stock, got hold of and title to nearly all the best lands of the country. After the early settlers had passed away, the richest families and the richest citizens were of this race. And to-day, nearly all the old families who have been distinguished either for talents or wealth are descended from the old Covenanter stock. And what is true of Tennessee is believed to be true of nearly all the Southern States.

Long after the Revolution the Covenanters from Ireland still continued to come into Eastern Tennessee. They were all Protestants (generally Presbyterians), well educated, and many of them comfortable in point of property. I never knew one who was not reasonably well educated. In the course of time they almost universally became possessed of considerable property—enough to make them independent.

It may be asked, if the early Covenanter set-

---

* Haywood says that in 1768, 1769, 1770, all mercantile trade in North Carolina was in the hands of Scotch merchants, who lived in great style. The members of the Council were chiefly Scotch, and the members of the Assembly also. New edition, 50, 51.

tlers were generally so well educated, why so many of their descendants in the Southern States are to-day illiterate. Several answers can be given to this question.

1. Population in the Southern Colonies, before the Revolution, and in the States for a long time afterward, was so greatly scattered and diffused over that great territory, that a general system of common schools was well nigh impracticable. There was and there could be no concentration of effort and of means for this purpose. Unfortunately, as I suggest elsewhere, the township principle of local self-government, one of the main sources of the growth and glory of New England, was never introduced into the South. The result was that in the course of time, common education in remote districts was from necessity neglected, and the grandchildren of these educated Covenanters often grew up in comparative ignorance.

2. The Southern States, with inconsiderable exceptions in a few of them—those admitted into the Union since the adoption of the Federal Constitution—have derived no benefit from the provision made by Congress for the support of common schools, which set aside for this purpose every sixteenth section of the public lands, and by a later act gave an additional section. The reason

is obvious: When that law went into effect, there were no public lands in the older Southern States, and therefore the law had no force in them. These States had patriotically, but most unwisely and inconsiderately, for themselves, surrendered to the Nation, for the common good, all the territory belonging to them respectively, without reserving any part of it for the education of their own children. Virginia gave up a princely domain in the North-west, making no provision for the education of her own people. The result has been, the children of that State, from generation to generation, have grown up in ignorance, while in the North-western States a splendid system of education has been built up, founded on the land grant of Congress, originally the bounty of Virginia.

3. Slavery, if not positively unfriendly, never gave the cause of general education a cordial support. Perhaps this was because it was thought that a large educated, reading, thinking population of non-slaveholders was neither safe nor desirable in the midst of a slave population. Perhaps, also, the large slaveholders who had to pay for the education of their own children any way, generally having to send them away from home for that purpose, were unwilling to be taxed to

pay for the education of the children of the others
who had nothing.

While the influence of the Cavalier has always
been, and justly, too, very considerable in the
South, owing to the prestige of a great name and
splendid virtues, it is indisputable and undeniably
evident that a much larger race, with equal natural capacity, with higher culture as a rule, and
with greater enterprise and energy, scattered
through all the Southern States, and with marked
influence in most of them, could not have been
overshadowed by the smaller one, confined mainly
to one State.   The mere statement of the proposition, without elaboration, is sufficient to demon-
strate its correctness.   The larger and the greater
race has not been lost in the smaller one.   Neither
Cavalier ideas, nor thoughts, as has been generally
assumed, have given form and shape and color to
the institutions, the policies and the public opinion
of the South.   It has been the ideas and thoughts
and the genius of that greater and more numerous
people, the Covenanters, that have accomplished
this.   So quiet and earnest have they been in effecting this noble work and mission, that the world
had almost forgotten until recently that there was
such a people.   Even their descendants, in very
many cases educated persons, too, seem to have

been ignorant of their own origin. The Covenanters have a history, but no historian. To obtain
any definite knowledge of this remarkable people,
it has been necessary to put together fragments
and scraps of history gathered from a multitude of
sources.*

The historians of the country have been almost
silent concerning them. Bancroft in his first edi-
tions gave only partial information about them.
Haywood and Ramsey, the early historians of
Tennessee—though the latter was honorably descended from a distinguished Covenanter ancestry, and was proud of the fact, and though nearly
all of our population were of this blood, and the

---

* About 1878, I undertook the preparation of a lecture on
the Scotch-Irish in East Tennessee, and, to my surprise, I could
find in American histories only slight references to this people.
There was no full, connected account of them to be found anywhere. While I was thus engaged, the little volume by the
Rev. J. T. Craighead, D.D., entitled "Scotch and Irish Seeds in
American Soil," made its appearance. . Ten years later, the
"Scotch-Irish Society of America" was organized in Tennessee, and it has published eight volumes of addresses from
prominent men all over the country, containing valuable material for the future historian. Recently, too, Douglas 'Campbell, in his valuable book, "The Puritan in Holland, England,
and America," has devoted one chapter to the Scotch-Irish in
America. It is to be hoped that he will take up this subject
in a separate work.

monuments of their deeds and of their courage could be seen every-where—are as silent about them as if no such people ever existed.

It is surprising, indeed amazing, how little credit the Covenanters have received for their great work in this country; how historians and public speakers alike have overlooked and ignored them, and how, until recently, they had passed out of the public mind, and were known only by tradition as a people that once existed, but which had been lost in the course of time. By many persons they have been confounded with the native Irishmen—a majority of whom were uneducated and of a totally different religious faith—who have poured in such numbers upon our shores during the last sixty or seventy years.

One reason, perhaps the main reason, why so little is known of the Covenanters, why they have received so little credit for their work, is that they were scattered over the whole country from Maine to Georgia. They settled no colony exclusively, and founded no State, as the Puritans and the Cavaliers did. They were in the absolute, the undisputed control of none. In each of the Colonies, if they were not in a minority, they could only work in co-operation with or in subor-

14

dination to the older people whom they found on their arrival. Thus environed, there was no opportunity for the manifestation of that individuality, for those high evidences of greatness which have distinguished this people in every part of the world. The nearest exception, perhaps, to the truth of the above statement is found in the later history of the Colonies of New Jersey and Pennsylvania, and in the States of Tennessee and Kentucky. And yet, neither of these was distinctively of Covenanter, as Massachusetts and Connecticut were of Puritan, and as Virginia was of Cavalier origin.

At the eighty-ninth annual dinner of the Pilgrim Fathers in New York, December 22, 1894, where as usual all the talk and all the eloquence were expended in praise of the Puritans and the Cavaliers, the gifted Henry Watterson (when his time to speak came), after speaking at some length of these races, said :

"Each was good enough and bad enough, in its way, while they lasted ; each in its turn filled the English-speaking world with mourning; and each, if either could have resisted the infection of the soil and climate they found here, would be to-day striving at the sword's point to square life by the iron rule of theocracy, or to round it by the dizzy whirl of a petticoat." . . .

"If you wish to get at the bottom facts, I do n't mind telling you—in confidence—that it was we Scotch-Irish who vanquished both of you—some of us in peace, others of us in war—supplying the missing link of adaptability, the needed ingredient of common sense, the conservative principle of creed and action, to which this generation of Americans owes its intellectual and moral emancipation from frivolity and pharisaism, its rescue from the Scarlet Woman and the mailed hand, and its crystallization into a national character and polity, ruling by force of brains and not by force of arms."

While Puritan Massachusetts was still overshadowed by the gloom of a narrow and cruel fanaticism, and Cavalier Virginia was still held in the iron grasp of an effete caste and lingering bigotry, the Covenanters were every-where from their pulpits and in their schools, quietly but effectively sowing the seed of toleration and of political and religious emancipation, and blazing out the pathway of the Revolution. They sounded the first notes of the war, and helped to fight its battles. When peace again came, they fixed the unfading impress of their advanced ideas and

strong characters on the institutions and on the
life and the thought of the larger part of the
country.

It was the people of Covenanter blood who
made the Southern States. Whatever these States
and the people of these States may be, whatever •
of good or evil there may be, in religion, in education, in science, in art, in invention, in literature,
in thought, in oratory, in statesmanship, or political
economy, whatever heroism and glory in war there
may be, these are all mainly due to the Covenanters. I will not enter into a criticism of the
political methods and political theories of these
peoples, but it must be strikingly manifest to all
candid minds that they have gloriously maintained
their theories and opinions, both in the forum of
debate and on the field of blood, with a skill,
a daring, an ability and prowess never excelled.
I would not withhold from the Cavalier just
praise for the share he has had in molding the
political and social institutions of the South, but
must deny that he is entitled to the chief credit,
or even to an equal credit with the Covenanter in
what has been done.

Though history has not recorded the work of
this people, the evidences of their deeds still remain. They have builded monuments, but put no

inscription thereon to tell who the builders were. They left monuments in the assertion and establishment of religious liberty; in first declaring for the Independence of the Colonies; for their share in the battles and the victories of the Revolution; in the large share they had in the framing of the Constitution of the United States, and in giving form to the national government; in organizing states and stamping the policies thereof with their own peculiar impress; in founding and building institutions of learning, and in maintaining every-where their lofty and pure principles of religion, morality, justice and honor, which constitute the true glory of any people.

If great names are the evidences of a great race, surely no people of modern times has surpassed the Covenanters, though too modest to write their own history. I name only a few: Alexander Hamilton, Patrick Henry, Thomas Jefferson, James Witherspoon, the Livingstons, the Clintons, James Monroe, Andrew Jackson, James K. Polk, John Bell, Hugh Lawson White, Sam Houston, the Rutledges, the Pickneys, John C. Calhoun, W. C. Preston, the Breckinridges, Zachary Taylor, James Buchanan, Stephen A. Douglas, Andrew Johnson, U. S. Grant, Chester A. Arthur, Rutherford B. Hayes, Generals Knox, Montgomery, Stark, Sullivan, Morgan, Howard, Sumter, Moultrie, Reed, Stuart, Martin, Wayne, Armstrong, Mercer, Marion, Rutherford, George Graham, Joseph Graham, Irwine, Davidson, Pickens, St. Clair, Lewis, Porter, Nash and George Rogers Clarke. Take six of these names, Hamilton, Jefferson, Henry, Calhoun, Jackson and Grant, and it would be impossible to find in our own annals, or in the annals of any other nation, in any one century of time, six grander names.

Wendell Phillips said: " Races are tried in two ways, first, by the great men they produce; secondly, by the average merit of the mass of the race."

Surely the race must be a remarkable one that could produce so many eminent men.

I have thus far been speaking chiefly of the Covenanters in the South. I have shown that it has been their ideas and their acts principally, and not those of the Cavaliers, which have dominated and controlled that region, and molded and given form to its institutions. Their influence, however, has not been limited to the South. Their sons and daughters have gone out to the North-west and have spread all over that vast region, even to the far-off shores of the Pacific. Whenever a new State or territory was opened to settlement among the first to enter it have been the descendants of the Covenanters, vieing with the Puritans in the eager race of life and in planting civilization in the wilderness.

The Southern Covenanters formed only a part, though the larger part, of that people which came to the Colonies. Pennsylvania, Delaware, New Jersey, New York and New England, as we have seen, all had a share of the influx of the Covenanters in the eighteenth century. They spread westward with the great stream of settlers who filled that vast region. They, too, have had a part in the glory of the marvelous development and growth of the West. The Covenanter has not been lost there in the Puritan, nor absorbed by him. They have retained every-where their marked individuality. In every State and territory, they can be found to-day, the equals of the Puritan in all the essentials of manhood, and fully as advanced in culture and civilization, and in all the arts of peace and refinement.

In the entire framework of Southern society and Southern ideas, the characteristics of the Covenanters appear. Time and association and affiliation with other races, especially with Cavaliers and Huguenots, have modified to some extent his original traits. But there runs through Southern life a manifest undertone of Covenanter thought. The steadfastness of purpose, particularly in reference to all questions of religious faith and practice, is a remarkable illustration of the well-grounded character of this stock. This fact stands out as one of the marked distinguishing peculiarities of the Southern people. They believe and worship as their forefathers did. They preach the same faith that was preached one hundred years ago, only with less of the terrors of the law. I refer to those who are of the Calvinistic faith. Many have gone into other churches, and in the course of more than a century, the Covenanter blood has been largely intermingled with that of other sects. But the faith and the practice of those who still adhere to the grand old church remain substantially as in colonial days. The strictness of former ideas alone has yielded to greater liberality. On all the vital moral questions of the time, the lofty standard of the old Covenanters, slightly relaxed, is maintained to-day.

There is a high conservatism in religious thought in the South which is remarkable. It is found only in that quarter. No new theories, no new creeds, no new religions make any headway. They soon perish and die out. Infidelity, agnosticism, spiritualism, universalism, and the infinite number of new theories prevalent in New England, find no home in the South. The extreme austerity of the early Covenanter may possibly still cast its gloom over their descendants. Be that as it may, they are unquestionably a thoughtful, serious, conscientious people. There is, as a general rule, but little of the light-hearted merriness, the sparkling gayety of the frolicksome Cavalier of Old Virginia, or of Old England about them. The men are earnest, ambitious of fame and power, fond of home, knightly toward women, and jealous of their honor.

The women are modest, graceful and lovely. They shrink from notoriety, and have no desire for the applause of the rostrum, or the lecture platform, or to mingle in the exciting scenes of a ward election, or to propagate new religions. They are content to be as their mothers were: virtuous, gentle, the guides of the family, the counselors of their husbands, the ornaments of society; adorning the home, and reigning supreme in it with queenly grace, filling the atmosphere around them with the sweet fragrance of love.

Nowhere in the world is public sentiment more exacting as to ethical and religious observances and practices. It demands propriety of conduct,

15

honorable deportment, and purity of life. Things
sacred — home, religion, the Sabbath, and the
church—must be treated with the most reverent
respect. Herein appears the spirit of the pious
old Covenanters. Some things are deemed too
high even for the State to touch. They are placed
beyond its reach, and are excepted out of the
powers of government. The perfect freedom of
religion from the first was guaranteed against all
human power. This was largely the work of the
Covenanter. While the legislature of Virginia, as
already shown, was struggling with the old bigotry
of the State, abolishing tithes and an established
church, imposed upon the people by the early
Cavaliers, the Covenanters both in that State and
in New York, were demanding, and successfully,
too, an absolute divorce of Church and State.
This was the yoke which had galled them. This
it was which caused them to quit their peaceful
homes in Ireland, and to seek the wilderness,
where they might found a free church. Never
did men come with higher, purer, nobler purposes.
And never did men consecrate themselves to their
great work with more heroic or with sublimer
courage. It sometimes seems to be forgotten that
the Covenanters, quite as much as the Puritans

and the Pilgrims, fled to this land to escape persecution.   And it is true of them, as it is not of the
Puritans, however it may be of the Pilgrims, that

> "They left unstained what there they found,
> Freedom to worship God."

CHAPTER VI.

THE COVENANTERS AND THE PURITANS.

The Puritans—Grand history since 1761—Important influence
in England—Revolution started by Covenanters in Scotland—Puritans leave England—Covenanters a better race
than the Puritans—Comparison of two races—The Church
in Massachusetts—A cruel theocracy—Enumeration of
cruelties, with authorities cited—Annals stained with narrowness and crimes—Whipping, banishment, and hanging—Children condemned to banishment—Intolerance—
Reason given for cruelties and intolerance—Reasons ex-
amined—Not the best educated people in the Colonies—
Massachusetts as the leader of liberal ideas—Caste—Difference between Puritans and Covenanters as to liberal
ideas—Massachusetts as to the equality of men before the
law.

The length of this discussion forbids that I
should do more than glance at the Puritan, the
other principal race justly credited with having
contributed largely toward founding our institutions. No one will deny their claim to a large
share in the glory of having made this great country what it is. The only question is whether they
do not demand, and have not received, too much
credit. In considering this race we meet a history,
since 1761, replete with noble deeds and abounding
in distinguished names. It is luminous and re-

splendent in statesmanship, in oratory, in letters, in science, and in all the industrial arts. Its material, like its intellectual development, has indeed been marvelous. Unlike the Covenanters, while it has accomplished splendid things, it has had its historians to proclaim its deeds. Pens and tongues, many in number and of unquestioned ability, have made known to the world all that the Puritans have done. The land rings with their praise. There is not a corner of the world in which it has not been sounded. And let not a single laurel that hangs on the monuments of their greatness be taken away, for their achievements are a part of the common glory of our country.

I freely and gladly acknowledge that the Puritans had a large agency in establishing political and religious freedom in England. Unquestionably, they helped to set in motion currents of thought, which, though small at first, finally became so broad, so deep and so resistless that they swept away the monarchy, and up-rooted many hoary wrongs and iniquitous practices. But the Puritans were not alone in the accomplishment of that, the most important of politico-religious revolutions, and the forerunner of all subsequent ones. They were powerfully aided by the Separatists, or the Independents, and by the dissenters and non-conformists of all kinds, as well as by many lovers of liberty who were attached to no particular ecclesiastical organization.   Unquestionably the action of the Scotch Covenanters, or Presbyterians, previous to this time, in resisting successfully both the King and the Church of England, in their determined efforts to fasten on the people of Scotland a liturgy and an ecclesiastical polity they hated, had a great reactionary influence on the still incipient movement in England.   We have already seen, according to Macaulay, that the successful revolution which began in Scotland, in resisting the enforcement of the liturgy, spread to England, and that to it the latter country owed her freedom.

Campbell says: "James drove out of Scotland many of the leading ministers; they took refuge in England, to disseminate there the doctrines of the Presbyterian Church standing above the state, and in time their teaching developed into action."

So it appears, that while the Puritans and the Separatists (the Pilgrims), were struggling for reforms in the established Church in England,— the former remaining in the Church and seeking to correct its abuses, and the latter going out of it and insisting on its entire separation from the State,—the Covenanters of Scotland had already achieved these reforms by the revolution spoken of above. They had previously virtually driven the Church of England from their country. This revolution in England, as we have seen, resulted in the overthrow of the monarchy, and in the end in the establishment of civil and religious liberty. Before this was accomplished, however, many of the Puritans, as well as Pilgrims, suffering under persecutions and despairing of any relief, had abandoned their country, and found an asylum in the wilderness of Massachusetts.

It is not my purpose to run an extended parallel between the Puritans and the Covenanters. Both were great races, and both performed a leading part in making the republic what it is. But one race has been applauded and glorified in all the literature of the century, while the other has been neglected and almost forgotten. Let justice be done to the one as well as the other. It must be kept in mind that the early history of the Puritans in this country, is far from being so bright as that after 1761.

I venture to state, and I believe I will be unqualifiedly upheld in my opinion, in the face of all that has been written and sung in praise of the Puritans, that the Covenanters, taking their beliefs, their practices, and their acts as a basis of estimation, were all in all, a better and equally as great a race of men as the Puritans. For want of space, I can only briefly cite a few facts to sustain this opinion:

No one will question the statement that in devotion to the cause of civil liberty, both in the Colonies, and in their respective native lands, the Covenanters were always as true as the Puritans. Both were faithful, with singular unanimity, to the cause of Independence in the days of the Revolution.

But in reference to religious liberty, the two races were as unlike in the Colonies as light and darkness. The history of one is shadowed by narrowness and often by crimes; the other reflects only the soft mellow light of toleration. It is freely admitted that the Covenanters, at one time in Scotland, at an early day, were guilty of persecution. But they never were so in Ireland, where they went prior to the settlement of the Puritans in Salem. In the Colonies they nowhere advocated or practiced intolerance. They had felt the iron yoke of bigotry on their own necks, and in the bitter school of experience and suffering they had learned the beauties of forbearance. They denounced the union of Church and State. They favored no religious tests of any kind, holding to the sacred right of religious liberty. No person was persecuted on account of his religious opinions. Quakers and Baptists were neither banished, nor whipped, nor hanged for their heretical opinions. No one was ever hanged by them for witchcraft. The sacred precincts of the family were never entered to prescribe the kind of garments women should wear, and what they should not wear.*

They did not attempt to exercise an immediate supervision over the conduct of individuals in the community in any of their private or public acts and relations. They had no selectmen, or overseers, who were required to have a special oversight over the education, the behavior, and the occupations of children within their jurisdiction, and "to see that they were taught to read, to understand the principles of religion, the nature of the laws; also to spin, to knit and to weave; a fixed quantity of 'lining, cotton, or wooling' being required to be spun by each family."† They had no sumptuary laws fixing the price of all articles sold in the community; "of all labor, and of all servants' wages."‡ Heavy fines and penalties were never imposed by them on men for non-attendance

* Bryant's History, Vol. II, 62.   † Id., 64.   ‡ Id., 62.

at church, or for failing to observe fast days. All
of these were Puritan practices or requirements.

In short, the Covenanters, though ·austere and
rigid in all church observances, never deprived
the citizen of every vestige of volition, of every
exercise of freedom, of every attribute of manhood,
nor made him the blind slave of a most narrow,
bitter, and intolerant theocracy.

The church in Massachusetts was the State. The
magistrates were only its willing instruments to
execute its fanatical and intolerant will. In all
the Colony there was not, and there could not be,
a free conscience or a free man. Even the magistrates and the ministers of the gospel were enslaved
by their own dark devices. They were made
gloomy by the pall of superstition and bigotry
which they threw over their own minds and consciences, as well as over those of their deluded followers. In all the Colonies, so far as personal and
religious liberty was concerned, no picture so somber and forbidding, so absolutely without one
gleam of light, can be found as that of Massachusetts and Connecticut in their earlier days. The
press was muzzled, and all free speech suppressed.
No man dared to censure or condemn the church,
the ministers, the State, or the magistrates, or to
utter one word of independent thought contrary to

the policy of those in authority. And no man could vote, or was even a citizen, unless he was a member of the church. Was this condition any thing short of the most abject slavery? Freemen of Massachusetts! They were slaves all—slaves of a terrible and austere fanaticism, and of a cruel theocracy.

Even the town meetings, the boast and the glory of Massachusetts, were most undemocratic. The people took part in them, it is true; but as Prof. Alexander White pertinently asks: "Who were the people?" He answers: "The members of the Congregational Church. Voting and office-holding are (were) limited to church members. The right of citizenship is (was) decided by the church register. The form of the government is (was) a *theocracy*. The real rulers are (were) the church officials, more intolerant of personal liberty than Archbishop Laud himself. . . . Hardly one-fifth of the adult population belonged to the Congregational Church, but this oligarchy of 'saints' ruled the rest with a rod of iron."*

On all these points, it would be easy to multiply authorities, but I shall quote only historians who are in deepest sympathy with the Puritans.

---

* Proceedings of Scotch Irish Congress, 1892, Vol. IV, 121.

Thus, Douglas Campbell, who is their constant eulogist, says:

"On the other hand, Massachusetts showed her English origin by the exhibition of some less pleasing characteristics. She was the only one of the Colonies, except Connecticut, in which witches were put to death; she alone hanged the inoffensive Quakers, and her records tell the worst tale—with the exception of those of Virginia—regarding the atrocities committed on the Indians, who were robbed of their land and constantly kidnaped and sold as slaves to the Southern planters. So, too, she, longer than almost any other Colony, clung to the censorship of the press, and longer than almost any other state to the union between the State and the Church." *

Again he says:

"They" (the Independents under Cromwell) alone stood up and demanded liberty for others, as well as for themselves. They alone proclaimed the principle of religious toleration, denounced the witch-madness, and asked, with Milton, that the press should be left untrammeled."

"But with these novel ideas the founders of Massachusetts, who had left England at an earlier date, were, in the main, unacquainted. At home

---

* Campbell, Vol. II, 414.

they had belonged to the established church. Their ministers were Episcopalians, who, until Laud began his persecuting rule, had been satisfied with Episcopacy. They believed firmly in a union of Church and State, and in the suppression of all schisms, provided *theirs was the church and the suppression of schisms was intrusted to their hands.*" * .

I quote from a distinguished son of Massachusetts, Charles Francis Adams:

" The offense, as well as the policy to be pursued by the government, was explicitly and unmistakably set forth by the chief executive and the presiding officer at the trial of Mrs. Anne Hutchinson, when Governor Winthrop said to her: .   .   . 'Your course is not to be suffered.   .   .   . We see not that any should have authority to set up any other exercises beside what authority hath already set up.'   .   .   . But Winthrop's words speak for themselves; and in the subsequent history of Massachusetts, the policy set forth in them was maintained and vigorously enforced by frequent infliction of the penalties of banishment and death. The public sentiment behind the policy, and which insured its enforcement, expressed itself in many forms." †

* Campbell, Vol. II, 413.

† Massachusetts, its Historians and its History, 13, 14.

In 1661, Samuel Willard said : " I perceive they are mistaken in the designs of our first planters, whose business was not toleration; but were professed enemies of it, and could leave the world professing *they died no libertines.*" *

Again. . . . " It is putting the case none too strongly to say that for nearly half a century, until 1680, religious conformity of a rigid character was in Massachusetts enforced by all necessary ecclesiastical and civil compulsion. During that period, the clergy was inquisitorial, the magistrates severe." †

" If in the somewhat arid as well as meager record of Massachusetts' seventeenth century utterances, there are any which, subsequent to 1637, favor religious toleration, or breathe the spirit of toleration, I am not familiar with them, and would much like to have my attention called to them." ‡

When we come to examine the results of this theocratic government in Massachusetts, we find that its annals are stained with narrowness, bigotry, superstition and crime. If there be in the history of civilization pages of darker crimes and cruelties against men, than those of this Colony, in the

---

* Massachusetts, its Historians and its History, 18.

* Id., 17.   ‡ Id., 27.

seventeenth century, then we must search the records of the Inquisition to find them.

Says Mr. Adams, reviewing this history, and evidently with no impartial mind : "Wholesale proscription, frequent banishment under penalty of death in case of return, the infliction of punishments both cruel and degrading, amounting to torture, and that regardless of the sex of those punished; the systematic enforcement of rigid conformity through long periods of time—all these things are a part of the record—and in these bad respects it is not at once apparent how the Massachusetts record differs from those of Spain or France or England."*

Again he says ; "But there that record is, and it will not out. Roger Williams, John Wheelwright, and Anne Hutchinson come back from their banishment and stand there as witnesses; the Quakers and Baptists, with eyes that forever glare, swing from the gallows or turn about at the cart's tail. In Spain it was the dungeon, the rack, and the fagot; in Massachusetts it was banishment, the whip, and the gibbet." †

This is the testimony of a Puritan and a Massachusetts man. I quote again his words: "During the forty years which immediately followed the

* Adams, 41, 42.   † Id., 34.

synod of 1637 dissenters and intruders were accordingly punished in the Colony, or expelled from the Colony, under the penalty of death in case of their return. Nor was the threat of this penalty an empty one." *

Here he quotes from Palfrey, a Massachusetts historian, who says: "The provision which threatened with death persons returning after being banished was no novelty in Massachusetts legislation. It had been resorted to over and over again through a course of years, and had never once failed of its intended effect." † That is, over and over again persons who had been banished on account of their religious opinions had been hanged on returning. In 1659 William Robinson, Marmaduke Stevenson, and Mary Dyer, all Quakers, were hanged on Boston Common under this very law. And the magistrates would not incur the expense of coffins for their burial, and so their bodies were stripped and thrown into a pit unburied.‡

No one can doubt the absence of the spirit of liberty in the Puritan as he reads one of the laws passed about this time (1658 or 1659): "That all *children* and servants and others *that for conscience sake can not* come to their meetings to worship, and

* Adams, 32; Palfrey, Vol. II, 471.   † Adams, 32.
‡ Bryant's Popular History, U. S., Vol. II, 193, 194.

have not estates in their hands to answer their fines, must be sold for slaves to the Barbadoes, or Virginia, or other remote parts." *

Under this law Daniel and Provided Southwick, son and daughter of Lawrence Southwick, who had been banished under penalty of death—two poor children with no property—were condemned to be sold into slavery, and would have been sold, but no shipmaster in Boston would transport them. †

Read this order directed to the marshal, signed by Edward Rawson, secretary : " You are to take with you the executioner and repair to the house of correction, and there see him cut off the right ears of John Copeland, Christopher Holder, and John Rous, Quakers." ‡

Men and women were tied to the cart's tail and scourged from town to town. This happened also in New Hampshire, which then belonged to the jurisdiction of the Bay. Three women preaching in Dover were driven from constable to constable through several towns, receiving ten lashes in each town. This was in cold weather in December, 1662. " Josiah Southwick, an elder brother of the

* Bryant's Popular History, U. S., Vol. II, 190.

† Id., 190.   ‡ Id., 190.

two Southwick children, for returning from banishment, was whipped through Boston, Roxbury, and Bedham, and cast off into the wilderness." *

Says Bancroft: "A fine was imposed on such as should entertain any of the accursed sect," . . "and a Quaker, after the first conviction, was to lose one ear; after the second, the other; after the third, to have the tongue bored with a red-hot iron." †

Look on this remarkable picture of 1692: Cotton Mather, the greatest of Massachusetts divines, excepting Jonathan Edwards, sitting on horseback at the foot of the scaffold denouncing a brother minister, George Burroughs, who died before his eyes for no other crime than a denial of belief in witchcraft.‡ It was shocking to hang people because they were accused of being witches, but to hang them for unbelief in that miserable delusion was superlatively monstrous.

The foregoing acts of cruelty are given to illustrate the spirit of Puritanism in New England. It is most natural that its historians should pass over this phase of that remarkable people as lightly as possible. But Mr. Adams, from whom I have already quoted, frankly admits the truth of the

---

* Bryant's History U. S., Vol. II, 190.
† Bancroft's History (15th ed.), Vol. I, 452.
‡ Prof. Alexander White, Ph. D., in Scotch-Irish Congress, Atlanta, 1892, Vol. IV, 122.

record, so far as the naked question of religious intolerance is concerned, taking good care, however,
to say but little about the shocking crimes perpe-
trated in the name of religion. He says: "The
question of religious toleration was, so far as Massachusetts could decide it, decided in 1637 in the
negative. . . . But it is curious to note from
that day to this how the exponents of Massachusetts polity and thought, whether religious or historical, have, so to speak, wriggled and squirmed
in the presence of the record—' shuffling,' as George
Bishop, the Quaker writer, expressed it in 1703,
'and endeavoring to evade the guilt of it, being
ashamed to own it. So that they seldom mention it
to any purpose even in their histories.' They did
so in 1637 when they were making the record up;
they have done so ever since. There was almost
no form of sophistry to which the founders of Massachusetts did not have recourse then, for they
sinned against light, though they deceived themselves while sinning; and there is no form of sophistry to which the historians of Massachusetts
have not had recourse since, really deceiving themselves in their attempt to deceive others." *

That is very candid and explicit as to the fact.
But I am not sure but that Mr. Adams " wriggles "

---

* Adams, 12.

a little himself when he comes to explain the cause of this very extraordinary condition of things in Massachusetts under Puritan domination.   If I understand him, he attributes all the narrowness of the theocracy of Massachusetts to the narrowness of the prevailing religion—Calvinism.   It may occur to reflecting minds free from bias and partiality, and entirely removed from the influence of what he calls the "*filio pietistic*" feeling, that the logical inference is that the narrowness of their religion arose from the narrowness of the minds of the professors of that religion.   Calvinism did not make William the Silent and the people of Holland blind and intolerant, with whose example the Puritans were perfectly familiar.   There the principle of moderation was first proclaimed and practiced, even while the people were subject to the most remorseless persecutions by the Catholics recorded in all history.   Nor did Calvinism make the Covenanters in Ulster narrow.   There they lived a quiet, peaceful life of Christian charity, molesting no one, and seeking to molest no one, on account of his religious opinions.   With the example of these people, the early Puritans of Massachusetts ought to have been familiar, and some of them no doubt were.   Calvinism did not cause the Covenanters of Massachusetts, who came later, nor those of Pennsylvania, of Virginia, of South Carolina, of New Jersey, nor anywhere else in the Colonies, to be narrow in respect to toleration. On the contrary, they every-where demanded freedom for all religions. Calvinism did not make Cromwell and his army of Independents intolerant. On the contrary, they demanded liberty of conscience for others as well as for themselves. And Calvinism did not influence the Dutch of New York to be narrow and tyrannical during the sixty years they controlled that Colony. It is freely admitted that the Calvinists of Geneva and the early Calvinists of Scotland did persecute men on account of their religious belief; but this was at an early day, when it was the universal practice among all sects in Europe.

On reading Mr. Adams' most interesting little book, from which I have quoted, one can scarcely escape a slight suspicion that his hard blows were aimed at Calvinism more than at the men whom he arraigns for preaching and acting as they did in Massachusetts. He squirms, as he terms it, at their record, which he says they "can not escape," but seeks to palliate their bad acts by laying the blame on the religion and letting the actors escape. The world can not thus be deceived. The truth is, the founders of Massachusetts were a narrow, superstitions, stern set of men, and have left a gloomy record behind them, which no skillful use of words and sophistry can render bright or lovable. The most and the utmost that can be said in their defense is, that it was the fashion and the spirit of the age to persecute, the only exceptions being in the Netherlands, in Ulster, in England under Cromwell, and in the Dutch Colony of New York, and in the Colonies of Maryland, Pennsylvania, and Rhode Island, all being Calvinistic. Mr. Bancroft admits the offenses of Massachusetts, but by flowery, stilted rhetoric seeks to palliate and excuse them. He seems almost to consider them virtues.

Now, what did Massachusetts—the Puritans— accomplish for the world during its first century and a half of existence? Let Mr. Adams answer:

"As a period"—the theological period from 1637 to 1761—"it was singularly barren, almost inconceivably somber. It has left behind it a not inconsiderable residuum of printed matter, mainly theological, but of little, if indeed any, literary value. Than this residuum there can, indeed, ' be no better proof how fully Puritanism had done its destructive work.' . . . In the mother country that period was a fruitful season, for it began with Milton and closed with Johnson.' . . . In

Massachusetts, of writers or thinkers whose names are still remembered, though their works have passed into oblivion, Cotton Mather and Jonathan Edwards can alone be named. They were, indeed, typical of the time—strange products of a period at once provincial and glacial—huge literary bowlders deposited by the receding ice." *

"But it is a fact worthy of note that the Magnalia (by Cotton Mather) stands to-day the one single literary landmark in a century and a half of colonial and provincial life—a geological relic of a glacial period—a period which, in pure letters, produced, so far as Massachusetts was concerned, absolutely nothing else, not a poem, nor an essay, nor a memoir, nor a work of fancy or fiction of which the world has cared to take note." †

It is said these Puritans were highly educated, and it is sometimes said they were the best educated people in the Colonies. While denying the latter assertion, I admit the former, but insist that the fact only makes their case the worse by reason of it. If they had been simply ignorant fanatics, the world could make great allowance for them on account of that ignorance. But as Mr. Adams says: "They sinned against light." The leaders were educated in a double sense; they had learning, and

* Adams, 64, 75; quoting Doyle.   † Id., 67.

they had had experience in the school of intolerance and persecution. The latter, at least, if not the former, should have taught them wisdom, as it had taught the Covenanters and the people of the Netherlands a noble knowledge.

But were the Puritans of New England the best educated people in the Colonies? This has already been disproved in a previous chapter. There is no proof of it, except the assertion of their own too partial friends. It was with them, as it was with the Covenanters and the English of that day, and of this day also. Some were well educated, some were moderately well educated, and many were not educated at all, or very imperfectly so. The means of universal education did not exist in England at the time the Puritans emigrated to America. It would be remarkable to suppose that all who came over were well educated. They had had no better chance for universal education among them, than the Covenanters had had when they emigrated, nor even so good a chance. The fact is about this: The world has so long been accustomed to hear that the Puritans were the best educated people in the Colonies, and so little has been published, or even known about either the Covenanters in the Colonies, or their education, that it has been assumed that the former were

greatly superior in this respect to the latter.   I
have referred to the fact that of the three hundred
and nineteen Covenanters who applied to Governor
Shute, of Massachusetts, in 1718, for leave to settle
on the lands of that Colony, all signed their own
names to the petition except thirteen.   Can Massachusetts show a better record among her first
settlers?   It must be kept in mind that the Scotch
or Covenanter Colony planted in Ulster, by James
I, from which most of the Covenanters emigrated
to this country, were "picked men;" superior
men in all respects, and that education with them
was always a matter of the highest consideration
in Ireland, as it had been in Scotland.

It has been assumed and proclaimed a thousand
times that Puritan Massachusetts has been the
leader of the liberal and advanced political thought
of this country.   In the following extract from
Mr. Adams' book, we have a little boasting, a
little "ancestry worship," as he styles it.

"In that field" (in the field of political activity)
"Massachusetts was always at home—it enjoyed
an easy American supremacy which even its ice
age did not wholly arrest.   And now when the
struggle against superstition had drawn to a close,
that against caste came again to the front, with

17

Massachusetts still in the van. Indeed on this issue, in 1837, as in 1635, the proper and natural place for the Puritan Commonwealth was in the van. It stood there: indeed it was the van.*"

Again, he says:

" The record, opened at Plymouth in December, 1620, closed as a distinct and independent record in April, 1865. That long struggle for the recognition of the equality of man before the law, of which Massachusets was the peculiar and acknowledged champion, came to its close at Appomattox." †

The truth is, from the beginning " caste " was in higher favor and more regarded in this than in any of the Colonies, except possibly in Virginia. The distinction between the " better class "— those " above the ordinary degree"—and those of " mean condition," was expressly pointed out and declared by the General Court in 1651. Under the law enacted by it, regulating the kind of dress to be worn, and other things, magistrates, civil and military officers, persons of education and employment " above the ordinary degree," those who were worth two hundred pounds, and those whose estates had been considerable, but had decayed,— all those in a word called the better class, were

---

* Adams, 105.   † Id. 107.

exempt from the operation of these sumptuary
laws. But the court declared most earnestly,
almost pathetically, its "utter detestation and dis-
like that men or women of mean condition, educa-
tions and callings, should take upon them the
garbe of gentlemen, by the wearing of gold or
silver lace, or buttons or poynts at their knees, to
walke in great bootes; or women of the same
ranke to weare silk or tiffany hoodes or scarfes,
which, though allowable to persons of greater
estates, or more liberal education, yet we can not
but judge it intolerable in persons of such like
condition." *

On this point I quote Mr. Adams, who says:

"The magistrates talked of the 'common people,' and one code of criminal laws applied to them,
while another applied to the gentry." †

This was the way Massachusetts, in 1651, "led
the van, was the van, indeed," in its war against
caste, and in its struggle for the "recognition of
the equality of men before the law."

Another author says on this point:

" The New England Colonies were republics, but
not democracies. Most of them had state churches;
their suffrage, though broad, was restricted, and

---

* Bryant's Popular History United States, Vol. II, 63.
† Adams, 9.

among their people social distinctions were very marked.   When these Colonies became States they clung, with true English tenacity, to their old traditions, and looked with horror upon the leveling Democratic theories advanced in other quarters." *

Now look at the contrast as the learned author goes right on to say:

"In the South, on the other hand, with its large and influential Scotch-Irish (Covenanter) population, the natural tendency was to get as far as possible from the past.   Those men hated England as the New Englanders never did, and they also hated her institutions.   Their religion had taught them the absolute equality of men, and on this point they were in full accord with men like Jefferson, who had learned the same lesson from the philosophers of France." †

I quote again:

"Here, then, in this difference of race we may perhaps find an explanation of the fact that 'Virginia' (under the lead of the Covenanter, Patrick Henry, and the Hanover Presbytery), 'formerly the most aristocratic, became the most democratic of all the States; while Massachusetts, standing on old conservative ways, became the chief exponent of the opposing theories.   One thing is very clear—

* Campbell, Vol. II, 502.   † Id., 502.

from no English element of the population, except the Separatists' (not the Puritans, but the Pilgrims), ' would have come the ideas of human equality, freedom of religion, separation of Church and State, and universal suffrage.' " *

I ask the reader to carefully consider the three paragraphs just quoted from Campbell, the eulogist of the Puritans, as they prove all I have said as to the relative merits of the Puritans and the Covenanters. They also disprove the extravagant claim made by Mr. Adams, when he represents Massachusetts as sweeping forward triumphantly in the van as the champion of human equality before the law, from 1637 to 1865, at Appomattox.

I quote again from Mr. Adams on the same point :

" When the Constitution " (of Massachusetts) " of 1780 was framed, it yielded a grudging and reluctant consent to limited concessions of non-conformity, but it " (religious intolerance) " was then so potent and so rife that the framer of the instrument abandoned in despair the attempt to put his idea of religious freedom in any form of words likely to be acceptable to those who were to pass upon his work." †

---

* Campbell, Vol. II, 502.

† Adams, 97; quoting from John Adams.

Thus, while the constitutions of the several States were, during the Revolution, sweeping away nearly every vestige of religious intolerance, Puritan Massachusetts only granted partial toleration. Not until 1833 did she open wide her doors to all sects in worship. Thus, according to Mr. Adams, as late as 1780, religious intolerance was so potent and so rife that the framer of her constitution (John Adams) "abandoned in despair" the attempt to make religion free.

On the main line of thought, I submit one more citation:

"They (the Covenanters) contributed as little which was original to American institutions as did the Puritans of New England, but they were also willing to accept new ideas from other quarters, and they contributed elements to American thoughts and life without which the United States of to day would be impossible. By them American Independence was first openly advocated, and but for their efforts, seconding those of the New England Puritans, that independence would not have been secured." . . .

"They were the Puritans of the South—Calvinists in theology and republicans in politics. Not only did they contribute largely to the success of the Revolution, but it was mainly through their influence that after the Revolution republican institutions, unknown in England, were introduced into the South and West." *

Most reluctantly do I attempt to take from " Puritan Massachusetts " any of the honors she so gracefully and so complacently wears, won in the long contest over the abolition of slavery, but the truth of history compels my doing so. That State was not "in the van;" much less " was she the van " on that question until after 1836. The leading men of Virginia condemned the institution of slavery both before and immediately after the Revolution. In 1804 a number of Baptist ministers in Kentucky started a crusade against the institution, which resulted in a hot contest in the denomination, and the organization of the "Baptist Licking Locust Association Friends of Humanity." † In 1806 Charles Osborne began to preach "immediate emancipation " in Tennessee. ‡ Ten years later he started a paper in Ohio, called the " Philanthropist," devoted to the general cause of humanity. In 1822 a paper was started at Shelbyville (no State mentioned, probably Kentucky), called the "Abolition Intelligencer." §

---

* Campbell, Vol. II, 471.
† Life of Lincoln, in McClure's Magazine, Nov., 1895, 507.
‡ Id.   § Id.

Osborne probably went from Jefferson County, Eastern Tennessee, the same county from which John Rankin, the noted abolitionist, went, since his was the first name on the roll of the "Lost Creek Manumission Society" of that county in 1815.

Twenty years before Massachusetts took her stand at all on this subject, there were eighteen manumission, or emancipation, societies in Eastern Tennessee, organized by the Covenanters, the Methodists, and the Quakers of that region, which held regular meetings for a number of years in the interest of emancipation or abolitionism.* In 1822 there were five or six abolition societies in Kentucky.   In 1819 the first distinctively emancipation paper in the United States was published in Jonesborough, Eastern Tennessee, by Elihu Embree, a Quaker, called the "Manumission Intelligencer." In 1821 Benjamin Lundy purchased this paper, and published it for two years in Greenville, East Tennessee, under the title of the "Genius of Universal Emancipation." † Lundy was merely the successor of Embree. At and previous to this time, the Methodist Church in Tennessee, at its conferences,

---

* History of Tennessee, by Goodspeed Publishing Co., East Tennessee Edition, 882.

† See Autobiography of Benjamin Lundy, Hist. Tennessee (Goodspeed).

was making it hot for its members, who held, or who bought or sold slaves, by silencing or expelling them. *

On the other hand, as late as 1835, William Lloyd Garrison was mobbed in the streets of Boston, because he was an abolitionist.   About 1827, Benjamin Lundy could not find an abolitionist in that city.   In 1826, of the one hundred and forty-three emancipation societies in the United States, one hundred and three were in the South, and not one, so far as I know, in Massachusetts.†   John Rankin, the noted abolitionist of Ohio, who went from East Tennessee in 1815, or 1816—a Covenanter and from a Covenanter neighborhood—declared in the latter part of his life that it was safer in 1816 to 1820 to make abolition speeches in Tennessee or Kentucky than it was in the North.

In 1835, the poet Whittier, and George Thompson, the celebrated English abolitionist, were mobbed and narrowly escaped with their lives, in attempting to make abolition speeches in one of the towns of Massachusetts.

---

* History of Methodism in Tennessee, by John B. McFerrin, D.D.

† Autobiography of Benjamin Lundy; Wilson's Rise, etc., 1, 179.

In 1833, Governor Everett, of Massachusetts, suggested the expediency of prosecuting abolitionists.* Mr. Garrison said, in the first number of the Liberator, that he found in the North, "contempt more bitter, prejudice more stubborn, and apathy more frozen than among slave owners themselves." † It was estimated, in 1828, that in Tennessee three-fifths of the people were favorably disposed toward the principle of emancipation. ‡

In the Constitutional Convention of Tennessee, in 1834, a proposition was made to emancipate the slaves of the State, and it received over one-third of the votes of the members, and the favorable indorsement of all, those opposing it, approving the principle, but insisting that the time for that step had not yet arrived.‖

It is well known that Henry Clay commenced his political career in Kentucky by an effort to secure the emancipation of the slaves of that State. The fact is, the emancipation movement seems to have gotten its first start and strength

---

* Life of Lundy, 286.

† Centennial Address of Hon. J. M. Dickinson, Nashville, 1896.

‡ Id., quoting Life of Birney, 79.

‖ Journal of Convention.

in Virginia, Tennessee and Kentucky, though the Quakers of Pennsylvania made feeble efforts in that direction before the Revolution.

It thus appears that Massachusetts was a long ways behind even some of the slave states in the struggle for " man's equality before the law." It was not until 1836 that she led in the abolition movement.

CHAPTER VII.

THE COVENANTERS AND THE PURITANS—CONTINUED.

Noble traits of the Puritans—Their liberality and public spirit—Puritans and Covenanters contrasted—The Puritans a commercial people—Kept in a compact body—The Covenanters separated and scattered—Forced into interior—Covenanters build up a high civilization in the South—Their influence extends to North-western States—Were an agricultural people—No stimulus to authorship—Politics the highway to honor—Free thought and speculation in New England—Caste and social distinctions in Massachusetts—Puritans and Covenanters in the Revolution—The blood of the latter in the South—Their liberal ideas and influence in molding the thought and institutions of the South.

I now turn with pleasure to the more lovable and charming features in the character of "Puritan Massachusetts." In many respects she has a record of which every American citizen ought to be proud. In her educational system she stands pre-eminent. In great scholars and writers she enjoys an "easy supremacy" over her sister States. In manufactures and in all the industrial arts she has led in the wonderful development made in these directions in the last half century by our marvelous people. In all things material that minister to the

comfort, the convenience, or the happiness of mankind, in their homes, no people on earth excel the
Puritans of New England. They are nowhere
surpassed in thrift, ingenuity, energy, or enterprise. Their vast accumulations of wealth and
their stupendous adventures and enterprises prove
the truth of this statement.

The charitable institutions of the Puritans are
magnificent monuments of their liberality and public spirit, showing an enlightened sympathy with
struggling humanity. While close, exact, and calculating in their dealings, and careful in their expenditures, they are capable of the most noble liberality. Their charities, when the objects are
worthy, are as boundless as their sympathy with
want. Who can forget how nobly, how enthusiastically, how munificently all New England, and
especially Boston, under the lead of the noble Edward Everett, responded in 1864 to the cry for help
which reached them from the starving people of
East Tennessee after that region had been eaten
as bare as a desert by four large armies. All classes,
even the children, vied with each other in their
noble emulation in giving. They poured out their
money for the relief of the destitute, as freely as if
it had been water. If the climate of the Puritan is
cold and icy and dreary, his heart, when touched

with sympathy or a sense of duty, warms and glows in the presence of suffering as if filled by tropical heat.

In private life the Puritans have always been regarded as exemplary and upright, and in morals pure. In these respects the Covenanters were equally as much so. The Puritans were an industrious and frugal race; and so also were the Covenanters. The wilderness and wild savage foes had no terrors for the Puritans; equally as little had they for the brave and hardy Covenanters. If the Puritans came to the New World to plant there a pure religion, so also did the Covenanters. If the former was too manly to endure persecution, so also was the latter. If the one braved the perils of the sea and the hardships of the dreary wilderness for the sake of conscience and religion, the other did the same thing. There was no sacrifice made, no danger met, no heroic fortitude displayed, no sublime purpose manifested by the one, that was not as heroically made, met, and displayed by the other. If the conditions and the environments of the Puritans and the Covenanters had been reversed, it is almost certain that, in education, in the accumulation of wealth, in literary culture, and in general development, so grand and so successful in Massachusetts, the Covenanters would to-day hold the place now so proudly occupied by the Puritans. The two were not very unequal in any respect. Certainly the Covenanter was not the inferior of the Puritan in any element tending to the making of a great State or a great people.

Consider this matter for a moment. The Puritan, with equal advantages, had the start in a new country by one hundred and twenty-five years. He had a state all his own, and could form it as he pleased. The Puritan looked out on the ocean, which invited him to engage in trade and commerce. He built ships and ventured on its waters, and became a common carrier. He went abroad in search of trade among the nations, thus keeping up with the march of the world. He had the coast trade and the fisheries. He made gain and became rich. The people kept close together in compact settlements. The township system of local self-government, to which New England owes so much of its importance, secured concentration of money, energy, and purpose in any given direction. It made possible universal education. The town meetings stimulated free thought and inquiry. By them the inhabitants became a live, an alert people. In them they learned to argue, to debate, to question things, to govern. They started schools and made education universal.

On the other hand, the Covenanter, coming late, and after the whole coast, from Massachusetts to Georgia, had been occupied by prior settlers, was forced into the interior in all the Colonies. In New York, in Pennsylvania, in North and South Carolina, and in Georgia this was the case. There was no room for him to found a new State on the Atlantic coast. As a people, the Covenanters became scattered from the Kennebec to the Savannah. In Pennsylvania they were forced to the frontier. Finally driven across the mountains, they scattered over the western part of the State. In Virginia, following the frontier, they settled along the foot of the mountains. Crossing these they entered what is now West Virginia. Then in one line they passed on into Kentucky, and by another they went west of the Alleghanies, and spread over South-western Virginia, and down into what is now East Tennessee. In North and South Carolina the same process of finding homes in the interior took place. Finally, scaling the Blue Ridge, they came to the wilderness on the Watauga and the Holston. A part continued on three hundred miles further, through the pathless forests, to the Cumberland, where they founded Nashville and scattered over Middle Tennessee.

Thus the process of scattering, of separation, of

isolation, in a greater or less degree, took place nearly every-where. They had no ocean, no commerce, no fisheries, no intercourse with the outside world. They had no trade, except with near neighborhoods; no great navigable rivers on which to float their products; no markets; no great or even small cities, and no means of growing rich. They had the absolute control of no State, though with a large influence in a number of them, until Tennessee and Kentucky came into the Union. Under such conditions a thorough and universal system of education was impossible. The settlements were for a long time too sparse, and the people in too moderate circumstances for such an accomplishment. And yet, as we have seen, colleges and grammar schools every-where came into being. Education was kept alive, with a high standard of scholarship. Most persons of moderate means became educated.

While the Covenanters with pack-horses were toiling up the Alleghanies and the Blue Ridge, on their way to Tennessee and Kentucky, rich argosies, laden with the products of the Indies, were sailing home to Boston to make glad the hearts of her merchant princes. At the time the Covenanters were building their rude log-huts on

18

the frontiers, rows of stately buildings lined the streets of Boston, Newburyport and Providence. While the Covenanters in primitive wagons were slowly struggling through mud on their way to the nearest little village market, to barter and ex-change their domestic products, proud ships, laden with sperm and fish, grain and rum, were sailing out of the harbors of New England, on their way to the great marts of the world.

And yet, with all these disadvantages, the Covenanters in all the States south of New York, have gone on, quietly, modestly, and intelligently, building up a Christian civilization as perfect and as splendid in every respect as that of New England, and in some respects much more so. This work has not been confined to the old States. It has extended to the new States in the South-west and in the West. The influence of this race on the institutions, the thought and morals of these States, especially that of the more southerly ones, has been quite as far-reaching as that of the Puritans. The great States of Ohio, Indiana, Illinois, Iowa, Missouri and Texas, as well as California and Oregon, are largely the product of the brain, the energy, the enterprise and the capital of the Covenanters of the old Middle States, and of those south of them. This is notably the case as to Ohio, Indiana, Illinois, Missouri and Texas. In an able address delivered at Harrisburg, before the Scotch-Irish Congress, in 1896, Mr. William Henry Egle, M.D., spoke as follows on this subject:

"It was the same race of people." (the Scotch-Irish or Covenanters) " who, when peace came and independence was acknowledged, formed the advance guard of civilization. The winning of the West was due more to the Scotch-Irish, the landmarks of whose early settlement have been brought before you, than to any other race or class of men." *

I do not fail to recognize the share the Puritans have had in some of these States in this great work, but I utterly deny the justice of the claim usually made for them and by them. Nor do I refuse to the Cavaliers, the Germans, the original English, and perhaps other races, the honor of a hand in building up these States.

The legislature of Illinois of 1834, consisting of eighty-one members, was composed nearly entirely of " men of Kentucky, Tennessee, or Virginia origin, with here and there a Frenchmen." † The States of Indiana, Illinois and Missouri were

* Proceedings of Scotch-Irish Congress, Vol. VIII, 81.
† McClure's Magazine, for February, 1896, 234.

largely settled by the people of the States above named.

The reasons are obvious on a little reflection, why the Covenanters of the South have not built up a splendid literature, such as the Puritans boast of. They were at first, from the very necessities of their surroundings, an agricultural and a planting people. Commerce was impossible. There was no motive for settling in cities, and nothing indeed to build up cities. Country life became the fashion, as well as a necessity. Except the few who entered the learned professions, educated men sought a life in the retirement of a farm or a plantation. There, the stimulus, the hot excitement of emulation, existing in a literary atmosphere was entirely absent. There could be, and there was no contact of mind with mind, thought with thought. The enkindling influence of one mind, fired with a high inspiration, a divine afflatus over a kindred mind was entirely wanting. No hints, no vague suggestions, no gleams of great thoughts were caught from others and molded into fiction, or poetry, or history. Many a person of real power and genius has slept away his life, in vain, because he had not the contagion of fellowship, of contact, of emulation to kindle his own mind into a flame. No great literary center, such as Boston, attracted authors to it, to draw from each other inspiration—where minds were quickened and intensified by contact with other minds. Authorship was not the fashion in the South, and did not become a profession. At an early day politics became the highway to honor and power. This field seemed to suit the bent of the fiery, the impulsive, the enthusiastic Southern gentlemen. Here high ambition found its vent, and the fulfillment of its aspirations. Into that flattering, seductive field, ambitious young men eagerly entered as the way to honor. The impetuosity and the ardent spirit of Southern genius naturally led in that direction. There have been at all times talents of the highest order in the South. In statesmanship, in oratory, at the bar, on the bench, in the pulpit, in medicine and in war, this fact has been constantly and most signally illustrated for more than a hundred years. In these respects the· South can proudly challenge a comparison with any other region of our country. Authorship requires leisure, repose, libraries and freedom from care. Above all it needs fellowship, stimulation, emulation and a literary atmosphere. The Southern people had leisure and repose on their great plantations, but not the other requisites. They had no literary center, no literary circles, no incitement to authorship. They had no group of literary men, like Emerson, Bryant, Whittier, Longfellow, Holmes, Lowell, Bancroft, Prescott, Motley, Hawthorne, and Thoreau to inspire them with a noble emulation.

I have referred to the fact that the preachers of the Covenanter faith in the South (and it is true of nearly all other sects also) have always been and still are conservative in all their religious opinions, never having abandoned the creed of their fathers in any of its essentials. How different in Puritan Massachusetts. That State—indeed, all New England is more or less so—has become a hot-bed in which every religious opinion, every wild theory, every vague speculation, every shade of belief, hanging on the " ragged edge" of disbelief, finds a congenial soil in which to germinate, take root, blossom, and bear fruit. Like a huge pendulum, religious opinion has swung from one extreme to the opposite—from the rigid and somber orthodoxy of Jonathan Edwards to the liberalism of William Ellery Channing—from the strictest Calvinism, with good works and faith in Christ as the corner stone, to the doctrine of " the efficacy of good works and moral living " without Christ. This, however, is only one of the developments of free-thinking—the supremacy of reason. Every form of unbelief seems to be creeping into the religion, the thought, and the lives of that people. The work of destroying the monuments of the past has gone forward fearfully fast. It is well that some of them should be pulled down, but let those that are valuable be respected and spared.

From the very beginning, as we have seen, there has always been a tendency toward caste in Massachusetts. Her people were Englishmen. They had English ideas. Ideas of caste were a part of their heritage. I have already quoted one of their early statutes showing that a clear distinction was drawn between the "better class," those "above the ordinary degree," and those of "mean condition." Those of the latter class were not to wear the same clothing that the former did. Douglas Campbell points out, as we have seen, the fact that in New England "social distinctions were very marked," and that "when these Colonies became States, they clung, with true English tenacity, to their old traditions, and looked with horror upon the leveling democratic theories advanced in other quarters."

I refer to one more fact on this subject. In the discussion over the formation of the Federal Constitution, and during the twelve years following its adoption, the Federal and the anti-Federal parties were formed and came into being; the one, thoroughly democratic, was led by Mr. Jefferson; the other, led by Mr. Hamilton and John Adams, leaned toward a strong central government. Massachusetts and New England, following the lead of Mr. Adams, ranged themselves on the Federal side, while the Southern States followed the leadership of Mr. Jefferson. Massachusetts became a Federal State, while Virginia became thoroughly democratic.

In the great Revolutionary struggle, both in the advocacy of resistance and separation, and in fighting its battles afterward, the Puritans performed a glorious part. No one would take from them any of the honor they so nobly won in that time of trial. But the Covenanters were equally as patriotic and as ardent in the cause of independence, and as brave in battle. In the progress of the war the Puritans and the Covenanters (as well as many of the Cavaliers) stood manfully and bravely, side by side, through the long struggle, without wavering or dishonor anywhere, until independence was won. And though history has hitherto given to the Covenanters no distinct place, as a people, in that great contest, it must be that some future historian, with more ample material, will give them the high position they should occupy before the world.

Now, in conclusion, what has become of the five or six hundred thousand (or, if that is too many, of the four or five hundred thousand) Covenanters in blood who were in the Southern States at the date of the Revolution? Have they disappeared and been lost by the overshadowing influence of some greater race? What race? Has this strong, brainy, self-assertive—this great intellectual stock that has made itself felt wherever it has gone in any part of the world—has it silently disappeared and melted away in the South by contact with other and superior races? By no means. The blood and the splendid elements which formed the character and the life of the old Covenanters in their native land are still as potent as in the days of the Revolution. From generation to generation they still reappear, in as distinct outline as in the days of the absolute purity of its blood in the hills of Scotland. From generation to generation the manly forms, the great qualities, and the splendid endowments of the Prestons, the Henrys, the Randolphs, the Breckenridges, the Campbells, the Alexanders, the Witherspoons, the Blairs, the Jacksons, the Polks, the Grahams, the Doaks reappear in their descendants. Sometimes they appear among the Methodists; sometimes the Baptists;

19

sometimes the Episcopalians, and sometimes among
the Presbyterians. The Covenanters no longer exist as a distinct sect. The term "Presbyterian"
no longer signifies a "Covenanter." The old
Covenant no longer binds and holds them together.
They are scattered, and have mixed with other
races, but their splendid blood still pours its rich
current through the veins of the Southern and
many of the Western people. And so long as the
nation shall last, the blood of this wonderful stock
will exist, and make itself felt among men.

As the logical conclusion of the discussions in
the last four chapters, and the underlying thought
running through them all, it is affirmed as almost an
undeniable proposition that the advanced theories
and the liberal ideas, in reference to both political
and religious liberty, which, like threads of gold,
were woven into the institutions of the country
and the life of the people, and which gave them
their chief glory, were of Covenanter, and not
of Puritan or Cavalier, origin. This is so mani-
festly true as to religious liberty that the reader
has only to recall the facts already given in order
to command his ready assent to the truth of the
proposition. For it will be remembered that,
until after the coming of the Covenanters, there
was not one gleam of light in all the dreary

regions dominated by the Puritans and the Cavaliers. The despotism and the gloom of intolerance reigned supreme. A narrow bigotry and superstition cast their blighting shadows over the minds of men. Notwithstanding the bold and never-ceasing teachings of the Covenanters, from the day of their arrival in the country until they had aroused the storm of the Revolution, so difficult was it to induce the Puritans and the Cavaliers to relax their deadly grasp on the consciences of men, that eleven years passed away after the inauguration of hostilities in the Colonies before universal religious liberty prevailed in the Cavalier State, and nearly sixty years before complete religious emancipation was accomplished in Massachusetts.

The struggles for political and personal liberty are always easily remembered. The glare and the thunders of war are never forgotten. But the quiet, the persistent and the courageous warfare waged by the Covenanters, every-where and at all times, for the right of conscience, while it was effecting a revolution as important for the happiness of mankind as the great one settled by arms, did not appeal to the senses and the imagination of men, and hence it has been but little noted by speakers or by historians.

To prove the correctness of the other branch of my summary, or proposition, in reference to political freedom, it is only necessary to refer to the facts already given, to show the deeply-rooted ideas of caste and social distinction existing in the minds of the ruling classes, and in the society of Virginia and Massachusetts, previous to and at the date of the Revolution. These caste ideas and social distinctions did not prevent those favorable to Independence from doing their duty in the great contest of arms, but they did have a most important influence in shaping the institutions of the country, and in giving tone and coloring to its thought afterward. And in this second stage of the Revolution these Covenanters, dwelling in large numbers in all the States south of New England, with their liberal and advanced ideas, learned in their bitter experience of nearly two centuries, and with their creed of Republicanism, were ready to infuse their spirit and inject their ideas of equality into the constitutions, the institutions, and into the life of that vast region. Under this influence even aristocratic Cavalier Virginia became, as we have seen, the most democratic of all the States. Under this influence, also, the Constitution of Tennessee was framed, which was pronounced by Mr. Jefferson the most

republican in its spirit of all the American constitutions. And this same spirit pervaded the institutions of all the Southern States, excepting South
Carolina. I do not withhold from Mr. Jefferson
the high meed of praise he so richly merits, for
his magnificent work in behalf of liberal ideas and
republican institutions in Virginia. But Mr.
Jefferson was always a Covenanter in his opinions
as to political and religious liberty. Besides this,
we have seen that he would have failed in his
great reforms, except for the powerful aid he received from the Covenanters.

Nor do I ignore the teachings of Roger Williams, nor the liberal ideas of the Dutch of New
York, nor the conservative opinions of the
Quakers, nor the tolerant spirit of the Catholics
of Maryland, in accomplishing these great results,
but these were insignificant in their influence in
comparison with the widely extended power of
the great Covenanter race.

CHAPTER VIII.

PRESBYTERIANS AND OTHER DENOMINATIONS IN THE SOUTH.

The terms Covenanter, Presbyterian and Scotch-Irish—Covenanter blood in all churches—Presbyterians in the South—Have lost ground—Pioneer Methodists and Baptists—Methodists in 1770, in 1818 and 1890—Wonderful growth—Itinerant system—Remarkable growth of Baptist Church—Its record in behalf of political and religious liberty—Roger Williams—Numbers of the leading denominations given—Educational standard in leading churches—Usefulness of Christian Ministry—Civilizing influence of religion—Honor to the memory of Luther, Calvin, Knox, Roger Williams—Influence of Calvinism on the destiny of the world—Authorities quoted—Mission of Presbyterianism—Presbyterians in the South.

It has been very far from my intention to indulge in a sectarian spirit in any discussions in these chapters. And yet it is very difficult to write the history of the Covenanters, and especially to do them justice, without the appearance of sectarianism. Up to a period near the beginning of the Revolution, the Covenanters and the Scotch, and the Scotch-Irish Presbyterians, were so nearly identical, that to speak of the one was to refer to the other also. But in the course of time, and especially after the Revolution, by reason of intermarriages with other sects, the two terms ceased to mean the same thing. To-day they are by no means identical. These intermarriages between the Covenanters, or the Scotch-Irish Presbyterians, and other Christian denominations, have been so frequent that the term Covenanter may, or it may not, at this day signify a Presbyterian. The Covenanter in blood may be a Methodist, a Baptist, an Episcopalian, even a Roman Catholic, or a member of any other denomination. Nor does the term Presbyterian necessarily mean a Covenanter in blood. The members of the different branches of the universal church in this land, have so intermingled in marriage and blood, and so many have changed church relations, that no racial term will correctly distinguish them. The term Covenanter now simply means a distinct people and not a sect. Covenanter blood is plentifully diffused through all churches and sects, and all sects should be proud of the great deeds and the splendid history of that people.

There is not perhaps a Protestant Church in the South to-day without more or less Covenanter blood among its members. Take away all persons of Covenanter blood, especially in the mountain country of Kentucky, Virginia, West Virginia, Tennessee, Georgia and North Carolina, where so many of this stock originally settled, and in many cases the congregation would be nearly or quite broken up. This is as true of the Methodist and the Baptist congregations as of the Presbyterian. In some counties in this region settled by Covenanters, the Presbyterian Church has entirely disappeared, while the names of the people as unmistakably indicate the Scotch origin of a majority of them as would a district in Ulster. In all this large region, to which I have just referred, perhaps five-sixths of the Covenanters in blood are either Methodists or Baptists. Intermarriages have obliterated the original religious race distinctions.

Both the Methodist and the Baptist Churches, and indeed all other churches in the Southern States, are full of members of Covenanter descent, Many of the men in the Methodist Church who have been distinguished for piety and ability, and who have shed luster on that denomination, are known by their very names to have descended from Covenanter stock. I need only mention Bishop McKendree and Bishop McTyre, the Rev. Dr. McAnally and the Rev. Dr. McFerrin, all well known in the South-west.

The Presbyterians have relatively lost ground in the South, especially in the mountain region thereof, during the last eighty years. They were for the most part the first settlers in that region. They occupied the new towns as they were built up, and also many of the rich country neighborhoods. In these they erected their church edifices and their school-houses. To their churches at an early day immense congregations flocked from all the surrounding country, to attend divine services.* But as the population spread out from the towns and the valleys, into the hills and mountains, Presbyterian ministers were unable in all cases to accompany their members.

The result was, the pioneer Methodists and the Baptists came along and picked up these Presbyterian stragglers. The Presbyterian Church did not have the ministers necessary to meet the great and constantly increasing demands of a vast and ever-widening territory. However laborious they may have been, however active in missionary or evangelical work, and however earnest and energetic in planting new churches, it was impossible for a few men to meet the wants of all the new towns and new settlements which were constantly springing into being. Many settlements had to be

---

* The Presbyterian Church, in Greenville, Tenn., contained at an early day 1,000 members, while the town was a mere village and the population of the county small.

neglected, and were therefore lost to the Presbyterian Church. Many evidences exist of the energy, industry and zeal of the early Presbyterian ministers in the South, in the closing quarter of the last and in the early part of this century. But it was beyond human ability to do all things at once. It was impossible for a few men to establish and teach schools, conduct colleges, build churches, preach·at stated times, perhaps to several congregations widely separated, and also to follow the settlements in the discharge of ministerial duties as they rapidly spread southward and westward.

The Methodist Church was very weak in the days of the Revolution, and for some time afterward, in the Colonies. When Asbury came to this country, in 1770, he found 14 preachers and 371 members of his denomination. When he died, in 1816, there were 2,700 ministers and 214,000 members. In 1785 they numbered only 10,000, with 104 preachers.* In 1784 there were just 60 members in the Holston Circuit, which embraced nearly all of South-west Virginia, and all of upper East Tennessee.† In 1890 there were 30,000 ministers and 4,589,284 members in the United States.

---

* Methodism in Tennessee, Vol. I, 28.

† Id. 32.

Most opportune was the coming of Asbury, introducing a new system and a new element of spiritual life into the country. The Presbyterians had already occupied the towns and the densely populated neighborhoods, but the hills, the obscure corners, the mountain recesses had not been reached.

The Methodist itinerant system exactly met this want. Under it there was no point so remote, no corner inhabited by men so obscure or inaccessible, that was not reached. Earnest, fervent and aggressive, though often rude and uneducated, the itinerant preacher did his work bravely, patiently, joyfully. He soon arrested attention, found listeners, made converts, and then the rude church edifice arose in the wilderness. In summer's heat, or winter's cold, in rain, or sleet, or snow ; Sabbath and week-day alike, badly clad, shivering with cold, pinched with hunger, often ridiculed or reviled, and sometimes maltreated, the humble, faithful itinerant uncomplainingly went about, from year to year, as he was ordered by the bishop. It mattered not whether his lot fell in the older settlements, or in the wild mountains, or on the dangerous frontier, or across swollen streams, his duty was to go. There was no mountain so high but it was passed, no stream so broad or deep but it was crossed, no wilderness so lonely but it was penetrated, no inhabited nook or corner but it was found. The itinerant may not have been learned, nor eloquent, nor brilliant, but if he had the spirit of Wesley, if his lips had been touched by a live coal off the altar, men would hear, and many would heed him.

The machinery which put these itinerants in motion was moved and controlled by strong arms and intelligent heads, and directed by almost absolute authority. There was no friction in its movements. Nothing could have been devised more efficient for widespread conquests. Nothing could have so perfectly met the wants of a new and widely extended country. The growth of the Methodist Church is a marvel, as much so as the unparalleled growth of our republic. And yet it is exactly what ought to have been expected from such a system of church polity in a new country.

The growth of the Baptist Church is but little less remarkable than that of the Methodist. It, however, had an existence in England, in Holland and in the Colonies long before the Methodist Church was born. Its membership in the United States in 1890 was 3,712,468, only 776,716 less than the Methodists.

The record of the Baptists in the cause of political and religious freedom is a noble one. When the Baptists from England established their church in Amsterdam, in 1611, they declared: "The magistrate is not to meddle with religion or matters of conscience, nor compel men to this or that form of religion." . . . "But no words of praise can be too strong for the service which the English Baptists have rendered to the cause of religious liberty."* Under the general name of Independents, they formed a part of Cromwell's invincible army; they went down with the Commonwealth and afterward suffered relentless persecutions.† In the Colonies, Roger Williams was the first man to proclaim the great doctrine that conscience should be free. He protested to the bigoted Puritans of Massachusetts that "the doctrine of persecution for cause of conscience is most evidently and ·lamentably contrary to the doctrine of Jesus Christ." Such sentiments could not be tolerated at that day by Puritan Massachusetts, and he was accordingly banished to Rhode Island. There he established the first Baptist Church in the Colonies. In the Revolution the Baptists were faithful, as they ever have been

---

* Campbell's Puritans, Vol. II, 202.

† Id. 203.

to the cause of independence and the cause of human freedom.

While many of the Baptists, both preachers and laymen, are uneducated and ignorant, especially in the great mountain regions of the South, and some of them are opposed to education, they have done a great work in restraining vice and in lifting men into a higher life. Though the preacher may not always be learned, he is more so than most of his congregation. Though he may be ignorant, and he is often densely so, yet what he has to say is on the side of morality. He at least is capable of leading those who have had less advantages than himself, and he generally leads in the right direction. Better a feeble light than pagan darkness.

It may be of interest to state that Pennsylvania, in the North, with 216,248 members, is the great stronghold of Presbyterianism, while Tennessee takes the lead in the South, having 66,573 members. North Carolina is foremost among all the Southern States in Methodism, having 276,336 members; then follows Georgia with 275,784. Georgia leads all the States in the number of Baptists, having 337,241, followed by Virginia with 303,134. The Roman Catholics far exceed in number any other denomination in any single

State, having in the State of New York 1,153,650 members. In Massachusetts they have 615,072 members, and this is more than double the number of all the other denominations in that State The total number of Roman Catholics in the United States is 6,257,871; Lutherans, 1,231,072; Disciples of Christ, 641,051; Protestant Episcopalians, 540,509; and Congregationalists, 512,771.

While no exact standard of education, indeed, while no education at all is required in the Baptist Church, as a qualification for preaching, it must not be inferred that the great body of that denomination is indifferent to this vital matter. Such is not the case. As a denomination they are now as thoroughly alive to its importance as any other. They have many very learned and able men. In every part of the country their colleges and universities are found, some of them among the leading educational institutions of our land.

It is little to be wondered at that the Methodists and the Baptists outnumber the Presbyterians in the Southern States, even in those States and sections where the latter at one time had the undoubted ascendency, when all the conditions are taken into account.

The Presbyterians must have a high degree of scholarship, as well as a thorough training in theology, before he is allowed to officiate as a minister. These requisites are always insisted upon. It might, therefore, be expected that the candidates for the ministry would not be as numerous as they would be under a lower standard. And yet, strange to say, notwithstanding the long and expensive preparation which is necessary for an entrance into the Presbyterian ministry, the number of ministers in that church, in proportion to their respective membership, very decidedly exceeds the number either in the Methodist or the Baptist Churches. The ratio is about as four to three. The Methodist members (17 bodies) number 4,589,264; they have 30,000 ministers. Baptists members (13 bodies) number 3,712,468; they have 25,646 ministers. Presbyterian members (12 bodies) number 1,278,882, and they have 10,448 ministers. Total number of Presbyterians and Reformed (Presbyterians) 1,587,790, having 11,944 ministers.

It is perhaps not inappropriate in this connection to bear unequivocal testimony in behalf of the usefulness of the Christian ministry, even aside from the religious aspects of the question. One of the most potent agencies for the education of the people, whether in city or country, for the formation of healthy public sentiment, and for the dissemination of advanced thought is the pulpit.

It arouses by suggestion public thought and private investigation. It arrests and directs public attention. Sermons from Sabbath to Sabbath from the lips of men of real learning and ability, are equal to the best popular lectures. They direct the minds of the hearers into new channels of thought and investigation. As a factor in the development of modern civilization the vast influence of the pulpit can never be overestimated.

No one can understand the history of our country who does not study the history of the church. The pulpit has been in modern times one of the greatest instrumentalities, perhaps the greatest, in ridding the world of tyranny and oppression, both of body and mind. It first proclaimed the right of freedom of conscience. This by an easy step led to freedom of speech and freedom of political action. These are all related and flow from the same source. In these days, when so many scholars affect free-thinking, it may be well also to bear testimony to the beneficent influence, even as a moral agency, of the Christian religion in civilizing the world. Religion, in this sense, is civilization in its highest form. Education has done much in this direction, but it educates the head and not the heart. Education alone rarely makes men better. It sometimes

20

makes them worse. It furnishes greater power for evil. When men feel themselves absolved from all moral and religious restraints, they are apt to become demons. The scanctity of all law must rest on conscience and an enlightened public sense. Strike out all religious ideas, beliefs and creeds, from among the most advanced people on the globe, and they would at once turn back toward barbaric ideas and practices. Take away the security given by religion to the sacredness of home, the honor of women, the inviolability of property, and the repose of society, and soon law would become as impotent as mere gossamer. France, in her mad intoxication during the Revolution, abolished religion and the Sabbath, and rivers of blood flowed through the streets of her capitol. The magistrates of Rome understood the necessity of religion to restrain the wild passions of men. Gibbon, speaking of the different forms of worship of their deities, says: "They were all considered by the people as equally true, by the philosophers as equally false, and by the magistrates as equally useful."

The author of the Prince of India puts into the mouth of one of his characters these words: "The study of greatest interest is religion. I have traveled the world over, I mean the inhabited parts, and in its broad extent there is not a people without worship of some kind. Wherefore my assertion that beyond the arts, above the sciences, above commerce, above any or all other human concernments, religion is the superlative interest. It alone is divine. The study of it is worship. Knowledge of it is knowledge of God.*

Froude, the great historian, in one of his addresses, said: "Science only deals with generals, but religion goes to the heart of the individual; and so I feel that on this basis religion is impregnable against all the assaults of science. You may take my word for it that all that is grand, sublime, of benefit to the race, has come out of faith, and not out of skepticism. One lesson, and one only, history may be said to repeat with distinctness—that the world is built somehow on moral foundations, that in the long run it is well with the good, in the long run it is ill with the wicked."

In this connection the world can never sufficiently honor and revere the names and memories of Luther, Calvin, Knox and Roger Williams. At a later day, John Wesley taught the same great truths, upon which the fabric of our free institutions was founded by our fathers, and now so securely

* Prince of India, Vol. I, 119.

reposes in majestic grandeur.* Let the world honor
these great men, as benefactors of their race, for
what they so grandly achieved in making civil
and religious liberty possible for men.

But let the world forever remember that these
earlier great reformers opened and paved the way
for the work of Wesley and Methodism, by securing freedom of worship and freedom of conscience.
But for them this work would have been impossible. Let those who would criticize Presbyterianism on account of its rigid and austere theology
remember that to this great sect, in its various
forms, more than to any other human agency,
is due our political and religious liberty. Let
them remember that Presbyterianism came to the

---

* John Wesley, on getting the tiding of the battles of Lexington and Concord, thought that " silence on his part would be a
sin against God, against his country and against his own soul,"
and he wrote severally to Dartmouth and Lord North, saying:
" In spite of all my long-rooted prejudices, I can not avoid
thinking these an oppressed people asking for nothing more than
their legal rights, and that in the most modest and inoffensive
manner that the nature of the thing will allow. Is it common
sense to use force against the Americans? They are strong;
they are valiant; they are one and all enthusiasts—enthusiasts
for liberty—calm, deliberate enthusiasts. They are terribly
united; they think they are contending for their wives, children and liberty." Presbyterians and the Revolution, 17.

Middle Colonies and to the South, in the persons of the Huguenots and the early Covenanter settlers, first filling the country with schools and churches, and with the cry for freedom and a free religion. The Puritans, the Pilgrims, the Covenanters and the Baptists did the same great work for education and for freedom in New England.

It can be affirmed as a truth, that during the last half of the eighteenth and the first quarter of the nineteenth century, the Presbyterians did more for the cause of classical education in the old South than all the other denominations combined. Since the period I have named, other sects, and notably the Methodists, the Baptists and the Episcopalians, have also been doing a noble work in this direction.

Viewing Presbyterianism, or Calvinism, from an earlier period, we see that the fruit which it bore in the Colonies was the natural product of the seed sown in Europe.

"Calvinism," says Mr. Bancroft, "is gradual Republicanism." Froude calls "Calvinism the Creed of Republics."

"It was to Geneva," writes Mr. Villiers (quoted by Smythe), "that all the proscribed exiles, who were driven from England by the intolerance of Mary, came to get *intoxicated with republicanism,* and from this focus they brought back with them those *Principles of Republicanism* which annoyed Elizabeth, perplexed and resisted James, and brought Charles to the deserved death of a traitor." *

" Not merely in their representative assemblies," writes Hallam, of the preachers of Knox's school, " but in their pulpits they perpetually remonstrated, in no guarded language, against the misgovernment of the court and even the personal indiscretions of the king." †

Of the Scottish preachers Macaulay writes: " They inherited the republican opinions of Knox."

Carlisle says : " Protestanism was a revolt against spiritual sovereignties, popes, and much else ; Presbyterianism carried out the revolt against earthly sovereignties." ‡

King James said that " a Scot's Presbytery" agreed " as well with monarchy as God and the devil." ||

Bancroft said : " The political character of Calvinism," with one consent and with instinctive judgment, the monarchs of that day feared as republicanism, and Charles I declared it " a religion unfit for a gentleman," etc.

---

* Presbyterianism and the Revolution, 25.

† Id. 26.   ‡ Id. 34. || Id. 37.

" Show me," said Charles, " any precedent where presbyterial government and regal power were together without perpetual rebellions. It can not be otherwise, for the ground of their doctrine is anti-monarchial." *

" Calvinism was revolutionary," writes Bancroft. " By the side of the eternal mountains, the perennial snows, and arrowy rivers of Switzerland, it established a government without a king. It was powerful in France. It entered Holland, infusing an industrious nation with heroic enthusiasm. It penetrated Scotland, and nerved its rugged but hearty envoy to resist the flatterers of Queen Mary. It infused itself into England, and placed its plebeian sympathies in strong resistance to the courtly hierarchy. Inviting every man to read the Bible, and teaching as a divine revelation the natural equality of man, it claimed freedom of utterance. It inspired its converts to cross the Atlantic and sail away from the traditions of the church, from hereditary power, from the sovereignty of earthly kings, and from all dominion but that of the Bible, and such as arose from natural reason and equity." †

Motley says: "Holland, England, and America owe their liberties to Calvinists." Ranke, the great German historian, as well as D'Aubigné, say:

---

* Presbyterianism and the Revolution, 28.   † Id.

"Calvin was the true founder of the American government." Hume, Macaulay, Buckle, Froude, and Lecky all affirm that it was the stern, unflinching courage of the Calvanistic Puritan that won the priceless heritage of English liberty." *

Rufus Choate, speaking of the Calvinists, said:

"In the reign of Mary (of England) a thousand artisans fled from the stake at home to the happier States of Continental Protestantism. Of these, great numbers, I know not how many, came to Geneva. . . . I ascribe to that five years in Geneva an influence which has changed the history of the world. I seem to myself to trace to it, as an influence on the English character, a new theology, new politics, another tone of character, the opening of another era of time and liberty. I seem to myself to trace to it the great Civil War in England, the Republican Constitution framed in the cabin of the Mayflower, the divinity (theology) of Jonathan Edwards, the battle of Bunker Hill, the Independence of America."

Thomas Carlyle said of John Knox:

"That which John Knox did for his nation, I say, we may really call a resurrection as from death. . . . The people began to live; they

* Address of J. H. Bryson, D. D., before Scotch-Irish Congress, Vol. II, 101.

needed, first of all, to do that, at what cost soever.
. . . He is the one Scotchman to whom his
country and the whole world owe a debt."

Mr. Motley, speaking of the influence of Calvinism in the Netherlands, says:

"It would certainly be unjust and futile to de-
tract from the vast debt that Republic owed to the
Genevan Church. The Reformation had entered
the Netherlands by the Walloon gate (that is,
through the Calvinists). The earliest and most
eloquent preachers, the most impassioned converts,
the sublimest martyrs, had lived, preached, fought,
suffered and died with the precepts of Calvin in
their hearts. The fire which had consumed the
last vestige of royal and saceredotal despotism
throughout the independent republic, had been
lighted by the hands of Calvinists. Throughout
the blood-stained soil of France, too, the men who
were fighting the same great battle as were the
Netherlands against Philip II, and the Inquisition,
the valiant Cavaliers of Dauphiny and Provence,
knelt on the ground before the battle, smote their
iron breasts with their mailed hands, uttered a
Calvinistic prayer, sang a psalm of Marot, and
then charged upon the Guise or upon the Joyeuse
under the white plume of the Bearnese. . . .
To the Calvinists more than any other class of

men, the political liberties of England, Holland and America are due."

Mr. Buckle, not a Calvinist, but often very bitter against that sect, said in his history:

"In their pulpits, in their Presbyteries, and in their General Assemblies, they encouraged a democratic and insubordinate tone, which eventually produced the happiest results by keeping alive, at a critical moment, the spirit of liberty. . . . Much they did which excites our strongest aversion. . . .

"(But) what the nobles and the crown had put in peril, that did the clergy save. . . . They were the guardians of Scotch freedom, and they stood to their post; where danger was, they were foremost. By their sermons, by their conduct, both public and private, by the proceedings of their Assemblies, by their bold and frequent attack upon persons, without regard to their rank, nay, even by the very insolence with which they treated their superiors, they stirred up the minds of men, woke them from their lethargy, formed them to habits of discussion, and excited that inquisitive and democratic spirit which is the only effectual guarantee the people can ever possess against the tyranny of those who are set over them. This was the work of the Scotch clergy, and all hail to them who did it. To those men, England and Scotland owe a debt they can never repay."

Again Mr. Bancroft said of Calvin:

" He that will not honor the memory and respect the influence of Calvin, knows but little of the origin of American Independence . . . The light of his genius shattered the work of darkness, which superstition had held for centuries before the brow of religion."

These extracts reflect the voice of history.

The wonderful record and deeds of Presbyterianism in behalf of mankind, can never cease to call forth the enthusiastic praise of every lover of liberty. English, Scotch, Scotch-Irish, Dutch, Huguenot, Swiss and Colonial Presbyterianism, in all its various forms, with the never-failing aid of the humble Baptists, gave freedom to the world. It was the great reforming power of modern times. Its mission was to emancipate, enlighten, regenerate, educate and elevate the human race; to make it freer and better. It taught the humblest citizen to feel that before God and the law, he was the equal of every other man. It shattered and shivered the blind and hoary-headed falsehood of the " divine right of kings," and the sacredness of their persons, and forever exploded and annihilated the slavish dogma of " passive obedience and nonresistance" to arbitrary power. It broke the shackles of priestly superstition from the minds and consciences of men, and the iron fetters from their bodies. It made man as well as religion free.

And on this continent, the great reforming forces, the Covenanter, the Puritan, the Pilgrim, the Baptist, the Huguenot, the Dutch,—all of the Calvinistic family,—but always in the van, the Covenanter gave to the world the example of a "State without a king, and a church without a bishop." Whenever this sturdy Covenanter entered the wilderness, in Colonial days, he carried with him the Bible, the axe, and a gun, with a blazing torch in his right hand. And thus I would paint him, or chisel him in marble. I would represent him as St. Paul is painted by some of the earlier artists—as earnest, rugged, severe in aspect, with knit brow and pressed lips, with forward step and eye, and his face glowing with the light of faith and hope.

In concluding this chapter, I bear cheerful testimony, as all history does, to the steadfast devotion in all countries and in all places, of the Baptists to the cause of religious and political freedom. I also give the most sincere and enthusiastic praise to the Methodists for their wonderful work in the reformation of the world, and for their own advancement and progress in the cause of education. At the same time, I can not overlook the fact that the Presbyterians, above all other denominations, have been pre-eminently illustrious in the great cause of human rights, and in asserting and maintaining every-where on this continent, in every possible manner, the sacred right of the people to the enjoyment of a free conscience, a free religion and a free State. In moral living, they demand purity and exalted integrity; in the Christian life, self-denial, sacrifice and consecration. The highest and the most exalting principles of justice, honor, charity, rectitude and purity of life, from the earliest times, have been inculcated both in the home and in the pulpit. The fruit of the severe, rigid and uncompromising teachings of the Cove-nanter fathers—those stern, Godly men of the early days of the Republic—can be seen, after the lapse of a hundred years, in every community in which they held sway. They can be seen in the obedient observance of the Sabbath, as a holy day, in the strictness of family government, in the gravity and sobriety of the lives of the people, and in a reverent respect for all things sacred.

The record of Presbyterianism in the South is one of which that church may well be proud. In every great movement and work of the age, for

advancing the condition and the happiness of mankind, for lifting men up to a higher plane of living,
for ameliorating suffering and misery, in the great
works of charity and love, and in promoting a
Christian morality and a pure religion, that church
has always been foremost. And though it is out-
numbered by three other churches, yet in maintaining a pure and spotless religion, in all the
great works of reform, charity and education, and
in the great missionary work of evangelizing the
world, it can securely challenge a friendly comparison with the records of any other sect or
church in the United States.

INDEX.